www.articity.com
www.stephenpaulthomas.com
http://www.theclusternovel.com/
https://www.facebook.com/stephenpaulthomas.writer
https://www.facebook.com/TheClusterNovel

STEPHEN PAUL THOMAS

Death in the Stars

short story collection

copyrighted material

Stephen Paul Thomas: Death in the Stars
2014
Originally published in Hungarian:
Stephen Paul Thomas: Halál a csillagokban (2013)

Cover and inner design, graphics:
Istvan Tomasovszki

English Translation copyright © Istvan Tomasovszki

English Copy Editor:
Paige Duke
www.thepaigeduke.com

Printed format ISBN 978-963-89985-2-1

Publishing
Hungarian Version
© 2013, Articity Publishing and Media Ltd. Hungary
English Version
©2014, Articity Publishing and Media Ltd. Hungary
All text in this book © Tomasovszki István

This book is the intellectual property of the Author, Istvan Tomasovszki (writing under the alias of Stephen Paul Thomas). Any copying, digitalizing, republishing, quotes, internet publishing of any part or the whole text is prohibited without the permission of the Author.
www.articity.com
www.stephenpaulthomas.com
Printing:
Reálszisztéma Dabasi Nyomda Zrt. Hungary
General Manager:
Magdolna Vágó

All of the people in this book, living or dead, or possibly alive in the future are purely fictional. Any similarity with real names is a subject of science-fictional incident.

Therefore, it is clear that these short stories are fictional, this book is not a guidebook. Any matching with future similar events is the subject of the strange SF conjunction.

The universe of the Short Stories

Most of these short stories are in the Human Colonisation Early and Middle Period of the Solar System.

The author's other novels, Cluster (also published in English) and The Seed (currently undergoing translation) lead you into the same rich, flourishing, and adventurous period of the Human Colonisation, which may be realised someday.

Special thanks:

I would like to thank Paul and Margo for the outstanding help they gave me for my first two books in English. Without your help it would have been only a nice door stop.

Paige, I appreciate your never-ending motivation to correct my text and your suggestions to improve my English.

I thank God that I was never forgotten, and for his promises that He kept without compromise; this is the reason I'm free.

Index

I. Maximum Life Expectancy - 9
II. The Leader - 31
III. Down on the River of Souls - 53
IV. The Reanimator - 79
V. Nothing but Comet Dust - 99
VI. Parallel Juridical Process - 121
VII. Doomsday, 2241 - 145
VIII. The van der Bruck Incident - 163
IX. Soul Trap - 187
X. The Identity - 207
XI. Eastern-European Express - 231

For my son;
If one day you'll step out of the boat, you'll be never alone.

Dad
24/07/2014

I.

Maximum Life Expectancy

The nurse took the syringe and the vial from the shelf, soaked the liquid substance up, and stepped to the glass cover of the tubular medical container. She checked the name on the list: Laurence Bellanger. She is the patient who needs to have the wake-up cocktail injected. She carefully ran her finger along the line of the tubes—coming out of the patient's veins—until the end. She verified the switches and the connections, and then injected the cocktail into the tubes. In nearly three hours this lady would be awake, until then, the nurse would have time to prepare her bed in the high observation room.

Before leaving Madame Bellanger alone, she adjusted the patient's thin, grey hair and mopped up the perspiration from her forehead with a cloth. The disease had been eating Laurence's once nice-looking body from the inside out for years. Her limbs were covered with reddish patches, and her breasts were enmeshed in the net of burst capillaries. Her skin had flaccidly fallen into the valleys of the cheekbones, because the connective tissues had lost their flexibility. But even so, the face was in the best condition.

Life expectancy: 42 years—this was written in her file. She did not have much left of it. For her, the road would end soon.

The nurse adjusted the heated pillows, turned on the illuminant imitating the light of the sun, then left the room.

Soon the conditions started to change in Laurence's feeble body: the awakening infiltrated into her deep frozen dreams. Her veins enlarged, the blood heated to the level of the human body temperature. The dreams had become quicker as the comfort slowly increased. The rousing consciousness, which had been trying to hold these fantasy pictures back to have one more dream, knew that it would be its last dream.

But she may have a chance to go through one more dream.

And hopefully this would be the most beautiful one.

*

"Good morning, Madame Bellanger."
"No," said Laurence. She wanted to speak the word out loudly, but only a faint sigh came out.
"This is the wake-up call," she felt the touch of the nurse's hand on her skin. She had very soft and fragrant hands. Laurence wanted to prolong this moment for a while to enjoy this caress more. "Sleepyhead! You haven't had enough for 32 light-years?"

The nurse playful exaggeration was not totally covering the truth. Due to the spaceship's engine—which had bent the physical space—the trip had taken only one-and-a-half earthly years.

"But I want to finish this only last dream..." Laurence said finally, loudly when she was able to do so.

"You will finish at home. Be prepared, the ferry leaves for Earth soon!"

Laurence moved her fingers a bit. She felt there was no way back to the beatific dreams: she had to wake up. She wanted to catch that sentimental last scene that she had seen in the imaginary cinema of her mind. There she was still in her 20s, had just met with Jack, who was the only American student from the campus. They were at dancing, embracing each other. Finally the last dream ended with pleasing memories...

"What day is today?" she asked, more lively. She had opened her eyes a bit, looking through a thin gap of the eyelids. The rays of the artificial sun-like illuminant got into her yes and generated a burst of the wake-up hormones.

"Saturday, 10th of July, 2235. There is excellent weather in Paris. You will be assisted at the Charles de Gaulle by our colleagues. I think it will be an exceptional day," a natural optimism could be heard in her voice – or she was damned good to cheer up a patient with an incurable diseases on this *Hospice Spaceship*. It did not matter, Laurence got the message.

"May we leave?" asked the nurse. This would be the last time Laurence saw her beautiful smile. The Latin-American features of her face shone out nicely from the glowing white background. The picture of this sweet woman was frozen into her mind.

*

Her ferry arrived at the VIP terminal of the spaceport. She sensed the dinging noises of the neurotic traffic around her. She saw the glittering clusters of the ships hanging from the sky. Sluggish ferries headed off to the Moon Colony or to bigger spaceships, which would take their passengers to further destinations: to the Mars New Home or to the Jupiter's moon Europa Colony. A trip from Earth to Mars only took 2 days—she could not comprehend this. She had travelled with this incredible speed to the nearest Hospice Exoplanet, the D74X, too. She did it in a year and a half, there and back; meanwhile the 32 years had passed on Earth. She went on a sort of time travel—she flew to the future but aged only a year and a half.

The little flicker of hope, what she had when she left, came back again like a blazing flame on Earth.

She was pushed out from the ferry on a floating bed. The drops of painkillers came down from crystal clear bottles. Without them she could feel the unbearable pain that she hadn't had on the journey. It could kill her in a minute. The worst thing in this disease was not the unchangeable fate, but the intolerable pain that had accompanied it. She could not care about losing her legs, arms; if only this pain would go away! But the unstoppable and incurable disease—which started from a tiny bit of her finger and forced the living cells to die—had spread on, all over body. She hosted a slow and cruel killer.

"I am Jean-Paul Armangeaux," said the kind man shaking her hand, he must have taken the nurse's place. He was also a really good helper. He lifted her in a professional manner and placed her into the floating chair—Laurence did not feel any pain or discomfort. She remembered the time before leaving the earth: every movement was an exploding bomb of pain. Now she felt herself become almost weightless in a great, relaxed comfort, which might come from the new type of painkillers.

"Nice to meet you," Laurence was trying to smile, but it turned out to be just a good try: her facial muscles were immobile due to the long sleep. "If I were a bit fitter or younger we could even date."

"But Madame Bellanger, you are not only fit and young" said the man and headed off to the floating ambulance car "but very pretty!" The man was not just a perfect helper but he was a professional liar. But Laurence did not care about it. She enjoyed the compliment she could not have for years. Each of them was equal to a bottle of magical painkiller, even if this was only a polite gesture.

Paris had changed a lot. The unexpected marvels filled her with wonder. The boulevards of the ancient, bright city had sunk between the 120-floor skyscrapers—nobody used them anymore as a result of the growing traffic of the floating cars. The Eiffel Tower was still standing, although it had been chopped in half; it was on the top of a 150-floor building with its legs missing. But the light on the top of the viewpoint was still on.

The outskirts were still ugly, run-down, and drained. Although these dark, unlit slums had changed a lot too: they started to look worse than the favela of Rio, built on junk, made from tin.

"Only twenty-five minutes and we will reach the Dignity Hospice Center," said Jean-Paul, turning back from the front seat.

"Don't worry about me," waved Laurence. "If I have already been asleep for thirty-two years, then this half an hour extra will not shake me. Einstein said a few hundred years ago: time is relative."

The Hospice Center had become more modern and nicer, although it also provided luxury service before. If medical centers were rated like hotels, this one would have six stars by now.

The room she was assigned to was painted in the color of peach blossom with bright white azaleas. Small lights were imitating the flickering stars on the ceiling; a stone fountain let water run at the corner, and a small yellow patch—a canary—was trying to bring the spring into the room. It was pure hokum, what she did not like. They could switch off all the effect, the canary could be taken away too, but she did not ask it. She wanted to keep the nature in the room for her remaining days, even if it was just a fake parody of life. She had dreamt about the spring a lot, wanted to see it now.

"Madame Bellanger, I am so happy that you came back to us!" She immediately recognized Dr. Foucault. When she left he had started his career as a resident at Cell Biological Department. Now, at over fifty, his hair was a bit greyish. It was so good to see a familiar face in this rapidly changing world.

He drew a chair next to her bed and sat down, holding her hand.

"Today you have to have a big rest, but tomorrow," he said to her, "we will have a long chat."

"I've already taken an extensive, thirty-two-year rest," smiled Laurence.

"It was only one and a half years in reality, and your health status did not change," said the doctor, gently caressing her hand. "The post-hibernation indisposes the strong and healthy too, so you need to obey."

"I know," said Laurence with resignation, "I have to."

"Yes, you really have to…."

"But you have to answer only one thing."

"About the treatment and perspective we will speak tomorrow…."

"Not about that," said Laurence. "About my family. How are they?"

Dr. Foucault slowly tightened her hand to make her more secure.

"They are all right," he said with a warm glaze in his eyes.

But Laurence was still tortured by her doubts. What if he just lied? She felt that everybody wants to hold back the cruel truth from a patient with a deadly disease. Dr. Foucault must have known that he could not tell the truth to her without preparation. This could kill her immediately.

"We will speak about everything tomorrow. I have some surprises for you too," he added at the end.

"Right," sighed Laurence and shook his hand. "The aging suites you well, doctor. I love your nicely greyed hair."

The man left the room with a wide smile on his face. At least he could see that the sense of humor had not left his patient after that many years.

But a huge lethargy clouded her mind when she stayed alone. Every man forgot that she was still a forty-year-old woman. She was still younger than this handsome doctor. The disease made her old and wrinkled, how could she expect to be treated like a pretty woman, she thought. But she did not want to be treated as a living dead.

But new hope would rise tomorrow.

And hopeful dreams waited for her that night.

*

"Good morning, Madame Bellanger." His name was Frederic; it was written on his shiny nametag. This strong man came to her to lift her like fluff and put her into the floating chair. She had not known him before she left with the Hospice Flight, because he could have been in the nursery at that time. She wrapped her arm around his neck and inhaled the clouds of his masculine perfume. For a moment, she thought back to her marriage with Jack, or even earlier, the time of young loves. She travelled back to the time for a few seconds until she reached the chair.

"We start to move slowly, getting fit, to get back our muscles. The disease—as a taxman, who takes all—pilfered away a lot from the skeletal muscles. We have to stop it!" he said when he gently released her.

Laurence loved these strong men. They formed a robust shelter around her with their arms, and they blew the dark clouds away with their strong voices.

"With the new type of painkillers, you will be more comfortable and not addicted," he explained the newest medical invention to Laurence. He drove the floating chair through tortuous corridors. "These drugs were in the night-cocktail I mixed for you. You don't feel any pain, do you?"

"Oh, not at all. Only in my heart," answered Laurence. Frederic was puzzled.

"You can easily help on that without drugs," she added, "if you can tell me the truth about my family before we start the training today."

Frederic slowed down, and then stopped. The chair was still floating away driven by the force of inertia. He reached after her and turned back the chair:

"I know that you have to take a heavy burden on your shoulder. I know that you have gone through a lot of awful things, treatment and pain. But up to this moment you remembered everything fairly well. You remembered the fact that you had spoken with your family two months ago and they are all well. They only wait for you to grow strong, and then they will take you home."

I have been here two months already...

The words echoed inside her head, they sparkled around for an implausibly long time. Frederic could have been right: she remembered the greyish Dr. Foucault, the half-chopped Eiffel-tower, the lights of Paris, the spaceport De Gaulle, the ferry, the nurse with the Latin-American features....

But all of these might have been just memories or the side effects of these new painkiller drugs, she thought.

She let herself be driven through the unfamiliar corridors. According to Frederic, she had been here before—three times a week she had an appointment with Jacqline. She could swear on her life that she had never seen her before.

But she joined in the game: she pretended as if she were an old friend, smiled to each stranger she saw. Meanwhile, she struggled to hold onto the last cliff of normality, to the last clear memory: the kind face of the Latin-American nurse. If she could see her again, she could pick up a thread, which would lead her to the real world.

*

"Oh, you didn't lose that thread, dear Madame Bellanger," said Dr. Foucault, whose hair had turned into grey. He was the fixed point in this shattered story, he was alive and kicking, and last but not least, a very charming and attractive man. I wish I could have my brown, waist-length hair, she thought, and some flesh below my skin. I look like an old, dusted mummy from a museum of nature and science.

The doctor looked fabulous in his leaf-green office. Countless framed degrees and diplomas covered the wall behind him. Tiny plastic spaceships and ancient wooden models of sailing vessels thronged a small self. No family picture, no pretty blonde wife from a Caribbean honeymoon, while the doctor clasped his arm around her waist…. No picture of kids on graduation ball….

He has no family. What are the women of this future waiting for?

"The treatment we'd found against the Genetic Cell Disorder, how I can say…." He stopped for a moment.

Say however you like, just tell the truth, she thought.

"So it has a little side effect," he added. "In some rare cases, like yours, the drug can cause memory loss." It can be partial or total loss of some engraved bits of memories.

Laurence started to dig deeply into her defected memory to compose a reasonable question from the shattered pieces of bits.

"What did I miss? What happened from my arrival yesterday until we met today?"

Dr. Foucault turned back his diary.

"It is 19th of September today. You arrived here more than 2 months ago, on the 10th of July. From that moment we had successfully treated your symptoms, and this is clearly visible in your status: you became strong enough to come to my office on your own feet for the third time."

"Excuse me," Laurence stopped the doctor by lifting her hand. She could not believe what she heard. "This very morning I had to rely on the help of a strong gentleman to move into the floating chair. How can it be that I came into your office without any guidance? Strangely I don't remember your office at all, it feels like I'm here for the first time."

"No, it is not the first time," smiled the doctor. Laurence could fall in love with him if they were not in this chaotic situation. "And if I add that we met 3 times per week when you were still in the chair that is already more than 70 times."

Laurence stalled. She looked Speechlessly at the doctor. She felt that those remaining memories had broken into pieces and fell out through her ear to the ground.

"Look, dear Laurence," said the doctor, moving forward and gently brushing her hand. He had a silky soft touch surrounded with a chamomile cloud. "I suggest you let go of your worries, and try to relax a bit. Try to enjoy the evidences of your recovery! Look at your hand!"

Laurence had not taken care of her hands today— astonished, she pulled her fingers from the doctor's grip. Her skin was bright like the morning sky without a trace of dried, red rushes. She quickly checked her arm too by folding the sleeves of her robe up—the nets of burst capillaries had disappeared.

When she looked up, the doctor approached her with a mirror.

"Go and look into it! Bravely!" he said like a fairy. His eyes were like sweet chocolate bonbons.

She slowly turned the mirror and lifted it in front of her face.

She gasped…

"It is like a dream," she could only tell this silently.

"It is really like that," answered the doctor. Laurence could not hear what else the greyish, charming man said.

She was just staring at the face she had not seen for a long time.

*

After encountering a month of heavy work—when sometimes she had slid down the slopes of several odd memory blackouts—she was in front of the house. Laurence could barely discover the patches of the old district of Saint Germain, it had changed so exceedingly. The mental picture—what she could stick together from the crushed memories—still consisted of the garage and the porch, but in reality, they were just a dried out skeleton of wood. The old civil house had been reshaped. They'd attached a lookout terrace and parking spaces for floating cars, two of these sporty type of cars were hovering above her.

She'd asked Dr. Foucault not to notify the family about her arrival. The taxi driver had looked puzzled when she asked him to stop on the street level: nobody used the streets anymore. They are nice and clean, but empty—due to the use of floating cars. All buildings—and the life—pursued the high of the sky nowadays. There might not be a door at this level, or there is no doorbell. The fantastic Dr. Foucault gave her a communicator and programmed the number of the old house into it. He'd also told the taxi driver to stay until somebody opened the door. If there was nobody at home, he was to take Laurence back to the Hospice Center, and they would try to organize the surprise visit later on. The greyish, charming doctor liked her more and more, she thought. There might be something between them, which was more than sympathy.

She was grateful for the regained power—she ran to the door. She heatedly pushed the doorbell, thank God it was still there. Did it still work? If not, she would ask the taxi driver to lift her up to one of the terraces.

It could take some minutes to descend from up there, she thought, when she heard the fumble behind the door. Warm brown eyes appeared at the sight.

"Excuse me," said Laurence "my name is Laurence Bellanger. I'm looking for Jean-Francois Bellanger."

The eyes widened in surprise after a few sudden blinks, then the sight hole closed. Old manual key started to turn in the lock, and a young woman stood at the doorway.

"That Laurence Bellanger who had been flown with a Hospice Spaceship 32 years ago?"

This is it, Laurence thought, this is definitely the reality, and not another discontinuation of the mental time! She knows about me! She might be the wife of my son….

"Yes, I am," she answered. They glanced at each other for a moment. The age gap dissolved between them into the relativity of time.

"I'm Monique, the wife of Jean-Francois. Let me invite you into the house."

"It wasn't a good idea to bring you down to the street level" she said, already in the lift. "It was safe at your time, but not anymore."

"It never was," smiled Laurence. She did not care about the forever-changing world around her. There was only one thing she could concentrate on: she would see her son and, possibly, her grandchildren.

She counted on the science. She counted on the hope that they would find the cure for her disease, and she would watch her family members grow up, happily married, having children. Her husband—Jean-Francois's dad, the unpredictable American—had left when she was pregnant. She definitely did not count on that.

But, if everything went well, the first two whishes could turn out to be real soon.

The layout of the house had not changed a lot. She took a sentimental deep breath, and inhaled the smell of the memories from 32 years ago, which lingered below the modern, plastic walls, deep below in the layers of paints, where you can find the essence of the past.

"Have a seat. Jean-Francois has a busy day, he will be here soon. He works in a bank, where the working hours do not have much respect," said Monique. She kept a bit of distance, which was understandable after Laurence had just fallen into her life. "A cup of coffee or tea?"

"A tea would be wonderful, dear Monique," said Laurence. She wanted to dissolve the uncomfortable tension that came from the strange effect of time travel. She started to count again, as she did before, but the never-ending losses of memories made her count again: when she left, her son was four and a half, now he is 36 ... *Oh, Jesus! There are only 5 years between me and her son! It would be great if they could take this oddity easy...*

She was excited to see the first reaction of her son. She'd rehearsed this meeting with her beloved son many times, had imagined the way they would hold each other. He was still her small boy despite that he had a wife and maybe children. Through the time she was away, the Hospice Center took care of him—it was included in the price of the treatment, and they had done a great job—they'd educated him and brought him up. He earned a good job, which means he did not inherit the Genetic Cell Disorder, she thought.

"He's here. The driver of the bank just pulled beside the terrace right now," said Monique, with a big pot of steamy tea in her hand, made from fragrant green leaves. She placed it onto the small table, pushing away a pile of magazines. "I'll run to tell the good news," she said and disappeared behind the terrace's door. The curtain softly drifted away and Laurence could see the parking lights of the floating limousine. A tall, well-dressed man stepped onto the floor, waving goodbye to the driver. Monique rushed to tell the news, excitedly gesturing with her hand.

Laurence stood up with a teacup in her hand, straightened herself, and gently adjusted her hair, trying to show the best form to her son. The moment had come.

The man, who stormed into the room, had familiar features, blond hair, a nice face and smile. But something... something was not right.

"Laurence, Granny!" he embraced her tightly. "Dear Grandmother!"

Laurence did not want to escape from the forgotten hug she loved so much, although she did not understand the situation.

"Grandmother?" she asked with embarrassment in her voice.

"Yes, I'm your grandson, Jean-Francois Bellanger, the youngest. I got my father's name."

Laurence tried to put back the cup onto the table, but the tea spilled out, drenching the old photo of her son and her she had just placed there. The tea messed up the ink of the print the same way as the old memories washed away from her brain. She desperately tried to hold anything up that was real in this world. But nothing was real anymore. The room started to turn around her. She grabbed the back of the seat. Monique jumped to catch her.

"And my son? What happened to him?" Laurence asked gasping hard.

Monique glanced meaningfully at Jean-Francois from the corner of her eyes.

"Laurence, Granny," said Jean-Francois softly, "they did not say in the Center what happened with him?"

"Unfortunately he inherited the disease and… " started Monique, but Laurence did not hear her anymore. She had fallen into the hole of her memories.

Back to where everything was still in order or even earlier.…

*

"Mother, mother…"

There was dead silence in there. The silence travelled back into the time.

"Mum, mum... wake up!"

The time between the silence and the voice became firmly short.

"Mum, please, wake up. Do you think she is all right?"

"She had no complaint this morning. I will check her."

Another long pause, mixed with touches and the sound of crumpled sheets, while hands turned over her.

These are still the noises of the hospital....

So the recovery was just a dream ... again.

Only death remained.

*

"Mum, mum ... wake up!"

"She had no complaint this morning. I will check her," said Dr. Foucault.

"The side effect of the new treatment is that she lost days, weeks, sometimes months from her life, although we suppressed the disease already." The doctor and the nurse tried to free Laurence's chest from the clothes twisted around her. She'd had a seizure.

"The drug erases all memories when it fixes the neuron cells. We expected this with the healing process, but not in this extent. But everything comes back in time."

"How old is she exactly—I mean really—now?"

"Nearly 42."

"God, I'm only 5 years younger than my mother!"

"Yes, almost unbelievable that time has this strange behavior," nodded Dr. Foucault and pumped some drug into the tubes coming out of Laurence's vein. "The marvelous factor of this time travel was that we had found the solution for the problem. She can live a long and healthy life now although the life expectancy was only 42 years."

"I understand. Could the seizures be a serious complication of the treatment?"

"I don't think so. I gave her an anticonvulsant, it will reduce the cramps and relax the muscles."

They silently watched the nurse when she adjusted Laurence's waist-long hair.

"She still has remains of busted capillaries and the red rush on the skin, but all this will disappear in few months."

"So you're confident?"

"Yes, absolutely. Your mother is a truly amazing woman. I have to admit that I admire her stamina. She suffered a lot…"

"Thank you, Doctor. I am convinced."

"And what about you?"

"I'm perfectly all right. I got the result of the checkup. There is no mutation in mine or in my son's gene."

Meanwhile the nurse finished the sheets on the bed. Jean-Francois gently squeezed his mother hand. Dr. Foucault watched them for a moment from the doorway, then silently left the room.

***

"Wake up, Madame Bellanger."

"No," she said stubbornly, as she said before. "I want to finish this very last dream."

"Enough of the dreams! This is the time for reality! The voyage is finished!" She was the nurse with Latino features and the gentle silk touch. The greyish-charming Foucault doctor had similar skin in her dreams.

She slept through the approach maneuvers while the Hospice Spaceship reached the orbit. The radiant blue crescent of the Earth was more beautiful than any dream. Laurence burst into tears.

"What's the matter, my dear?" the nurse wiped the tears off Laurence's face. She swallowed the rest of her tears.

"I really don't know which part was real…"

"About the dreams?' asked the nurse and gave a light tranquilizer into the infusion. "Here you can dream a lot. You can dream the best and longest dream you've ever had. Almost everybody has a dream here. But you can be sure many parts of your dreams can be true at the end. I can tell you the best part: they'd found the solution to your disease on Earth while we were travelling around outer space! The specialist will start your treatment tomorrow."

Laurence remained silent.

"You don't look so happy," the nurse gently stroked Laurence's face.

"I am happy, but not surprised. I know all this from my dreams. But there is something that I don't know: what happened with my son?"

"That, I'll tell you, Madame Bellanger," said a man in a white coat, and turned to the nurse. "Would you leave us alone, please?"

The grey-haired, charming Dr. Foucault himself was standing beside her bed. Laurence was relaxed by his gentle touch and fragrant hands again. He was still good-looking, with his grizzled temple.

"I have good and bad news about your son. I'll start with the good one: his beautiful wife, Monique, gave birth to their son. They called him Jean-Francois. So congratulations, you became a grandmother!"

He paused for a moment.

"I have to continue with the bad news. Your son inherited Genetic Cell Disorder. His maximum life expectancy was 38 years at the time we made the diagnosis. He'd boarded another Hospice Spaceship to an exoplanet, he'll pass his journey too. Two years ago we didn't have the solution for this disease, so he had to fly away to gain some time. He'll be back in 12 years, and I'm sure, that we will have a far better method, which will not cause the loss of memory that you might have experienced."

"I know," said Laurence, "the side effect of the healing process will cause loss of memories for days, weeks, sometimes months…"

Dr. Foucault looked surprised.

"Oh, you had prepared somehow on this long trip," he said, smiling at her.

"Certainly," answered Laurence. "And you know what? I'm prepared about you too. You're unmarried, you had no relationship, but you're a habitual seeker looking for the brown, intelligent woman I had been one day. Your office is green where we will meet three times a week. I admit I'll never reject you in any case."

Dr. Foucault shook his head in disbelief.

"You're truly amazing. Where did you get this?"

Laurence was finally completely sure that she had found the way back to the reality.

"From my dreams."

II.

The Leader

It was the same morning as a thousand times before. The artificial sun rose up behind his room, it broke sharply through the thin gap of shutters, painting bright lines of light onto the projector walls. The lines slowly climbed up to his eyelids and tickled them. The walls projected the scene of the sunny beach, the room filled with the sound of the roaring sea—the computer had even produced a smooth, salty breeze.

Aaron sat up in his bed.

No question, he thought, *this is the day*. He could not even sleep well through last night, he was so excited.

He jumped out of bed, avoiding the approaching dress-updroid, and ran to the wardrobe. It was forbidden to touch the clothes, but he didn't really care about that—he tore the door wide open and started to throw his stuff on the floor. He chose jeans coveralls and a blue baseball cap.

"A-a-ron must not select clothes for himself," said the robot, and grabbed the jeans with his pneumatic steel hand. It was a wheeler-type, not a humanoid. "Especially today when we go off the surface."

"C'mon, Mr. Armani, the sun is shining as always," said Aaron, although he knew it was only an illusion. But he was full of hope, as always, that the reality was not so far from the computer-generated images. "Let me choose today!"

"*Know you very well, Aaron, this is possible according to the protocol, not,*" said the droid with a sharp voice. His speech generator was an old piece of junk, making errors with the order of words, but he was still able to express that he did not want to open a dispute on this matter.

Aaron furiously threw his stuff down. Mr. Armani collected them all and replaced them on the hangers. After he had finished, he reversed back to the wall and turned his rectangular shaped eyes to the boy.

"After checking the schedule today, I have found out that you need to dress up in a sport clothes. *You understand have to*, that the rough material of the jeans is not suitable for sport, even if it is very fashionable for a boy, *you are like*. I would like to offer a soft, impermeable jumper with training shoes to you."

"Ok, if we are doing sports, I will let you choose," Aaron reluctantly accepted the droid's suggestion. "But why impermeable? It's raining again on the surface?"

The droid paused silently for a moment. He swapped the projected pictures with imaginary scenes from the surface. The beautiful sea had disappeared, replaced with dark racing clouds. Small drops of rain fell onto the camera lens, but in the background, a thin ray of light broke through the quilt of clouds.

"This must be the weather at the moment, I assume. In the absence of live images I can just make a good guess."

Aaron pulled his jumper up with real anger.

"I hate, I hate, I truly hate that it always rains when we go to the surface. I'm not able to spend a complete sunny day up there.

I'm not satisfied with this artificial sunlight. Why can't you make a weather-generator if you're so wise and clever?"

Mr. Armani made a half-turn and placed training shoes in front of the boy.

"We robots are clever only as much as you humans, who programmed us, are. *We to make developments able*, but the weather control is outside our capabilities. I am truly sorry, master Aaron," the robot eyes could not express sympathy, but there was artificial compassion in his voice.

Meanwhile Aaron had finished dressing, all Velcro fastened, and he stood in front of the door, as always.

"I am Aaron Sonnenfeld, ready to go onto the surface," he said the usual sentence. The door remained closed, so he repeated it again louder. The door did not move, so he angrily kicked as much as a teenager could. Then the door slid aside, and at the very same time all emergency lights turned on. The projected, imaginary scene of the surface disappeared from the wall, the sun-like illuminant went dark; only the weak orange safety light broke into his room.

"Mr. Armani, what is going on?" he turned to the dressing-droid, but the mechanical helper was immobile. Aaron found it strange that it was blocked, although all robots had their own electric source. The electricity had gone off before, but that time all robots stayed active. Strange. *Then this is something else*, he thought.

He cautiously looked out to the corridor. Nothing and nobody was there, just the flickering orange light reflected from the shiny-metal wall until the elevator. *Does the lift work?* he pondered. He slowly slunk to the elevator's door as if he was afraid that somebody would jump out of the pit. All lights were lit on the panel, meaning the lift was up and running. He pushed the call button, and happily noted that the familiar buzzing noise filled the pit behind the door. A few second later, the door opened.

Then he hesitated, feeling uncertain for the first time, because he had never been up there alone. He had been accompanied on his previous voyages by Mr. Morton or Mrs. Elden. He could go alone, it was not hard, but the huge freedom was so frightening. There was a dangerously big freedom up there, bigger than he had in his room.

But I have to go, he thought, *this day cannot finish this way*. The power would come back anyway, as it had always come back before.

Don't put yourself above the others, this was the slogan of the first level as the elevator went up. He passed this initial level when he was five, played and laughed a lot with his friends—the specialized, programmed child-bots. They were designed especially for him; the classroom was filled with same-sized chums and advancing rivals. *A lot of tasks and trials, oh, God*, he thought back in time. The sweet taste of success mixed with the almond-bitter of failure ... he had to use and bear both. Success could sometimes be more dangerous, as it could make you over satisfied.

He still came back to this place when he was already seven or eight, only for the feeling. He kept good memories from the other side of the door, but they had emptied this level when he turned nine. The elevator had never stopped here again. The time of games and play had finished that very day. Mr. Morton and Mrs. Elden handed over a significant message to him by closing the level: he had to take his study more seriously.

The next was the study level—with the slogan of *if you think you know everything, then turn to the unknown*. This was really hard at the beginning, he thought, remembering his suffering. The slogan became worn as he had scratched it a lot. He wanted to nullify and annihilate this level, because he did not want to learn—only play. The classroom was cold and empty—no more classmates and games. He could not talk to anybody but he had been flooded with rules; don't lie down on the table, sit like that, don't chew your pencil … he had swum in the rivers of rules.

Finally the teachers—especially Mrs. Elden—found the key to Aaron's soul filled with desire for freedom. He loved everything on wheels: something that was rolling, running on rails, pulled by horses, or had an engine. The instructors organized Aaron's study materials around transport. The motion meant everything to him. He wanted to move quicker than he could run. But down there he could not do any dangerous sports. He asked to have a scooter or a bike, but the teachers did not bring it. They said this request depended on the decision of the Leader.

Maybe today, he thought. Maybe today. Today was his birthday.

And, of course, the blackout. On this very important day.

The elevator stopped at the level of *New dreams, new challenges*, where he attended regularly nowadays, as he was fifteen. He stepped into the room with a feeling as if he were coming to the course. But this cosy sentiment disappeared as he noticed that the room was empty and dark due to the blackout. He could only see the edge of the objects; the tools of the mechanical department in the background, where he could build what he had designed. There were test tubes in the foreground—the materials of the experimental department—and the telescope was standing on a tripod on the left side.

He loved this "magic-eye", as he had called it when he was younger. The miraculous equipment could see the stars even from this classroom—which was deep in the ground. Aaron had no clue how it could be possible. Even if they were up on the surface, the sky was always covered with clouds. Mr. Morton, his history teacher, told him that the wars of old generations poisoned the

Earth with acid rain. This was the reason he could not go onto the surface for very long. It would take years until the deadly materials had decomposed and the level of radiation had gone back to normal. The endless radioactive dust and grime increased the formation of clouds and caused never-ending rains. Mr. Morton hoped that in the future they might see the sun much more than mere minutes.

He also learned that they lived on an island. Aaron's father had designed and built all robots to take care of his son before he left the Earth for a mission. His desire was that Aaron would be mature enough to join him in the army later as a pilot. There was a war out there, a war into which the Earth—and humankind—had drifted. This was all the information he got, although he wanted to ask more questions. But instead of getting answers, he was assured: when the time came he would actively participate in the battles alongside his father. *I have a lot to learn until then*, he thought.

The elevator would no longer move, so he had to find the way up on the emergency staircase in the half-light. They had an evacuation drill every week, so he routinely followed the marker lights built into the floor.

On the way up he passed the level with the slogan—*self-defence is a necessary force but not a selfish violence*. He would start this level in a few months. According to Mr. Morton, he would learn all basic mental and physical self-defence practices here. He had no idea about the mental part, but he greatly awaited the physical activity—as he loved all kinds of sports.

Inevitable truth about the weapons.

Hmm… Strange, ambivalent feelings invaded him when reading the slogan of the last level. He wanted and hated this level at the same time.

It was surely necessary to learn everything about the weapons as the Instructors included it in the program. If the Instructors found it necessary, then Daddy had the same opinion as Daddy programmed all the robots, including the teachers. There was a war out there after all, and all wars had been fought by weapons.

It was strictly prohibited to enter this level. He looked around: the corridor was empty, no sign of any cameras—although he was sure there was one hidden somewhere. *Ok, it doesn't matter,* he thought, *this is an exceptional situation.* He would enter, no matter how severe the punishment would be.

It surprised him that the room was filled with shining bright lights. There was no sign of the blackout that had made the whole complex look like a rabbit hole. All the equipment stood there on standby waiting for somebody to sit down beside it. A huge, semi-circular console invited the visitor to touch its button and study its screens. It was some kind of radar system—a modern version of those old ones in the ancient war movies.

He could see three islands indicated with three-letter abbreviations on the huge, wall-size screens. The most familiar name was AS2—he saw that many places—and he thought that could be his island, although nobody had told him this. The island to the north was three times bigger; the one to the southwest was the same size as his. He was truly shocked. He was not alone in the middle of the Big Water.

He slowly circled the console. *Fully armed*—these words had been projected on the screens. He counted: the same text was on all twenty-two. He randomly sat down in front of one, and he wanted to change the words via the keyboard. As he touched the keys the text changed to *Request Login*. In vain he entered all codes he had used on the previous learning levels, all of them raised the same error—*Invalid Entry*.

So this must be a very high-level system, much more important than any learning phase before, he thought. None of the older passwords were valid here, so it could not be his level. It might be his father's level, waiting on standby for him until he came back.

But why did they put the slogan above the door?

He got tired of the attempts. He left the room and went up the stairs to the exit hall. It was dark, but at least he knew it already. Aaron stepped to the locker and took the mask for the small oxygen tank, which could be attached to his belt. He sprayed all his uncovered skin with a protective material against the remnant of the radioactive dust, and walked to the exit.

It doesn't matter how big or long the punishment will be, I will go alone to the surface today, he decided. Today was his birthday; they would have to understand this.

As he approached the stairs, he noticed a rectangular platform in the background. There was a very familiar object on it, which grew more and more visible as he got closer and closer; Aaron could see the determinative horizontal and vertical lines together with the smaller slim and graceful details. He was not only in a hurry, but was running toward it.

The boy jumped on the bike with a huge smile on his face.

Almighty God!—the bike was real! Astonished, he gently ran his hand over the frame. It was a much more beautiful bike than he had ever seen in movies. The robots were on their mettle! And this cool colour—bright red—was fantastic! *Happy birthday, my little soldier, Dad*—was written in red above, on a panel hanging on the wall. *Oh, Dad, you always know my deepest dreams*, thought Aaron with a wide smile on his face.

He came off the platform to test the bike in the long corridor. First he could not find the balance, but then he got the hang of it. He sometimes skidded on the shiny metallic wall but easily pulled himself back with his elbow. *This corridor was created for practice*, he thought. He wanted to do some turns until the electricity came back, and would leave the base with Mr. Morton and Mrs. Elden, and—not least—he would be a professional biker when they came back.

But the electricity did not come back, and he had become a true rider in half an hour. Aaron enjoyed the long runs and the sharp drifts; amazed with the way it slid on the slippery metallic floors.
He pulled the handbrake, stopping in front of the stairs leading to the surface. The elevator was still dead, so if he wanted to go above, he had to carry the birthday bike up the seventy-four steps. *I am ready, let's go*, he goaded himself. If he waited too long the chance for a free ride would disappear.
In the end, it was easier than he expected to go to the door that led to the surface. The bike was light and made from alumagno alloy according to the markings on the frame.
As he pushed the door open, he got a wonderful surprise from the sun; it struck a thick beam through the heavy clouds, covering him with warm yellow light. *Especially for Aaron*, he thought; he could not imagine a better start than this.
The bike was totally amazing. He chose the south path covered with a rough surface. The wind cut into his face and he started to sing, letting go of the handlebar with both hands. If somebody had seen him they would have burst out laughing, because his

voice changed under the oxygen mask; it was as if he sang into a mug or a pot. He laughed and sang continuously beating the rhythm on the handlebar. His heart sped up to the rate of joy, and he wanted this day to be never-ending.

After half an hour of frenzied riding, he slowed down. He was not tired, but realized that he had to save some energy for the way back. There were a lot of immobile droids around. Aaron knew some of the type, but most of them were unfamiliar. He had no clue what jobs they did on the island. They were covered with mud from their caterpillar tracks to their heads. Wherever they worked they were under extensive use. Their outer shell was not shiny like the artificial skins of Mr. Morton and Mrs. Elden. It was fairly strange that they were deadly motionless, despite having their own power systems. The small check light of the reserve battery—which was built into their chest and used when the robots had some rest for reconfiguration—was out too. *So this is not an update rest*, he thought, *this is a collective paralysis. It is a robot disease.*

He'd been riding for another thirty minutes when he saw a sugarloaf-like building coming into view. The sun was covered by clouds so he could no longer see the shapes clearly enough in the monotonous grey. Aaron had never come that far before on foot, they didn't let him. He didn't know that there were buildings on the surface.

The sugarloaf was surrounded by paralysed robots. All of them faced the path leading into the ground near the building. They had gone into that underground chamber before the strange disease hit them. The path was occupied by their bodies, Aaron could hardly overtake them. At the end—near the entrance—he had to get off the bike and push it through the dense crowd of robots. They might have come out from a shelter or something, and headed off to work. When the power came back, he would have an answer for this too.

Aaron leaned his bike against a robot, carefully adjusting the handlebar into its mechanical arm. It would not fall over while he was away for a short exploration. The door was blocked by a square-shaped heavy-duty droid, so he climbed onto its shoulder with ease to jump down on the other side.

Inside there were more than a hundred paralysed robots in the shape of a paper fan. It took a really long time to squeeze through the small gaps between them, but he finally reached the inner door. Aaron hesitated—with a mixture of fear and curiosity in his heart—but he pushed down the handle.

On the other side, there was a huge space that could hold a complete mountain. The walls were supported by sky-high, undecorated but graceful pillars. The construction reminded him of the ancient churches of the fallen civilisations. In the middle of the enormous space there was only a metallic, tube-shaped, human-sized object; it looked like the sarcophagus of the Egyptian kings. There was nothing else there besides the deathly silence.

Aaron took off his mask. The instructions said he needed to wear it only outside, *why would it be any different here?* he thought. He slowly approached the shiny object trying to keep his steps as silent as possible, because every small noise generated a never-ending echo in this huge building. A bright blue light circled around the floor when he reached the sarcophagus. It surrounded him and the fascinating object, which induced slight fear in him.

He should not be here. Mr. Morton would give him a big punishment for this.

Or the Leader.

Or Dad, when he came back.

This thing in the middle definitely had a bad look. It radiated the feeling of passing; of death. They often spoke about death, it was brought up on every evacuation drill. *The time used for evacuation is inversely proportional to the chance of survival, and the number of casualties is directly proportional to the increasing time of evacuation*, he remembered. The sarcophagus was not like the drill, it was strikingly real. It was tangible, deathly cold, with rounded edges, without any markings, made from brushed, stainless steel, like the outer shell of the droids.

It was a creepy-cold metallic death.

"Aaron, don't be afraid!"

The voice struck him from nowhere. He lost his balance and drifted backwards, then slid a few meters back on the smooth floor to the edge of the blue circle.

"I am Dad." The blue light pulsed on the rhythm of the words. It was without doubt the voice of his father; he had heard it many times before in the video-messages. They had also spoken live on the two occasions when Dad was near a long range, interstellar transmitter.

"Dad, where are you?" asked Aaron, pulling himself together and coming closer to the tube. But this time he stopped a half meter from it. He did not dare to touch the metallic surface of the object yet.

"I am here with you in this room"

Aaron was shocked by the statement. He was puzzled, trying to look behind the pillars to see if his father was hidden somewhere there.

"You are dead and you are a ghost?" he uttered, horrified at the words. Something had happened to Dad on the way back. His father flew back to be with him on his birthday, but something terrible had happened and the droids did not want to tell him the bad news.

"No, no..." laughed Dad. That was definitely the familiar, joyful laugh that he had become acquainted with in the interstellar messages. Dad was always cheerful except when he spoke about the long perspective of the war.

"Please do not worry. I am perfectly fine. This is a *stasis-cabin*. I have to spend a certain small period in it to regenerate my body. I went through a lot of bad things in the battles, so it is time to recover now. And finally, I got some leave to spend time with you! Look!" he said, and Aaron felt that he had to go to the other side of the cabin to the source of Dad's voice. The cover of the tube became transparent, and he could see his father's face and naked upper body inside. His chest was covered with wounds, scars split by bullets and the energy weapons.

But it was him, alive, and he had come to see Aaron on his birthday!

"Did you like my present, the bike, my little soldier?" asked Dad with a waggish light in his eyes.

"Yes, Dad, it is wonderful. I learned to ride it so quickly," answered Aaron zealously, and he leaned over the cover of the cabin. "I am so happy that you came!"

"Me too, my Dear. Look at you, how big you are! A grown man already!" said Dad. Aaron shyly bit his lips.

"Now you go," he added, "it's getting dark outside. Tomorrow will be a great day; you will learn a lot of serious stuff. We will start on the *level of weapons*."

Aaron was surprised because he had to pass the *level of self-defence* first. According to Mr. Morton, he could not jump through levels if he hadn't finished the previous one. The ultimate knowledge could be taken only through the principle of gradualness.

But Dad knows better, thought Aaron. He programmed Mr. Morton, Mrs. Elden, and even Mr. Armani. What he said is always true. With this jump he could go to Starfleet even earlier!

"All right, Dad, then see you tomorrow," said Aaron, and hugged the cover of the cabin again. Dad pushed his hand to the transparent cover from inside, and Aaron did the same from outside. He wanted to push his hand through the metal just to touch Dad.

"Go, my little soldier!" smiled Dad. He had wonderful eyes. Aaron saw his own eyes reflecting back in them.

Aaron slid his hand down slowly as if drained by the infinite love. As he went out of the bright-blue circle, the lights went off. All that remained was the shiny metal, silent, tubular object.

When he left the building, the robots had gone. *So the power came back*, he thought. The bike was leaning against the wall; he jumped on it and rode back on the obscurely dark road. It would take another hour to get back to the base. He had ventured very far, but it had been worth every moment. He could speak with Dad. He would not expect any punishment; Mr. Morton and Mrs. Elden couldn't say anything, nor could the Leader, because his Dad would take over his education tomorrow.

After ten minutes of riding, he saw those lights from the right-hand side, down the harbour. They did not go in a straight line, as the robot ships usually did. The rays of bright light marched round and round as if somebody was using a torch, lighting the tortuous road coming up the hillside. They came exactly to him, the spot where he was standing, at the end of the stairs. Aaron could see three humanoid figures emerged from the darkness. They might be humanoid droids like Mr. Morton, they might be the captain of the robotic ships. He decided to wait and to join them on the way back to the base.

"You, up there, are you Aaron?" The shout thrilled him and turned his blood to ice. *They were humans!* He had never met with humans; he had only seen Dad on video until today. He was deadly frightened and could not jump on his bike to escape, as he suddenly planned. He fell on the side of the road and bashed his hand badly.

"You are Aaron, aren't you?" asked a tall boy, or young man, Aaron could not see his face very well in the gloom. *He is around nineteen*, thought Aaron, when the stranger came closer and held out his hand to help him on his feet.

"Jack Spears, North Island, AS1," he said as an introduction. "This is Kilian Breitner and his brother, Paul Breitner, from AS3, South-West Island."

"Aaron Sonnenfeld, ah…, I think AS2. But I don't know what it means. I start the level of weapons tomorrow with my Dad," Aaron said pulling the mask away from his mouth. The strangers did not have masks at all, so Aaron did not see the point in wearing his now.

The three boys looked uncomprehending at each other.

"Your Dad?" asked the older boy who introduced himself as Jack. "You have a Dad? I mean real, flesh and blood?"

"Of course," said Aaron self-evidently. "I have just spoken with him. He said we start the work tomorrow."

The three looked at each other again. Jack leaned forward embracing Aaron's shoulder. He was the leader of them, Aaron thought.

"Cool bike," said Jack, "I got the same on my fourteenth birthday. Same colour, same style."

"Did you get it from your father too?" asked Aaron, and picked his bike up from the ground. Jack helped to force the front wheel to the correct direction by holding it between his legs, and pulling the handlebar into place.

"We have to tighten this nut here," Jack pointed to the part he mentioned, but he did not give the answer to Aaron's question. "Let's go back to AS2, it is getting very dark now." They went up the hill together. The nuclear-proof entrance of the base appeared in the far distance.

"Was there a blackout here?" asked Kilian Breitner. His curly, red hair pushed aside from his forehead by the evening breeze.

"Yes, there was. All robots were paralyzed, although every one of them had its own power supply, according to what I knew about them."

"What did the Leader say about you coming so far alone?"

"I did not speak with him today. He had to give my birthday present to me through the communication centre, but he couldn't, due to the blackout."

"I see. So you could not speak with him, so you came directly to see him," said the boy named Paul, looking over his shoulder. He was the tallest and oldest of them, with a beard and moustache, which made him look more serious.

"To see him where?" asked Aaron.

"There, in the building you have been in until now. In the temple."

Aaron was puzzled. He did not understand anything.

"The Leader is in that building too?" he asked with an uncertain tone in his voice.

"*Too?* What do you mean, asking if he was there too?"

"I mean besides my Dad. He was the only human in that building, laying in a recovery-cabin in the middle of a huge hall."

The three stopped and looked meaningfully at each other again. Jack stepped forward as a good, implicitly appointed leader.

"I think it is time to learn about weapons and start the real work on the final level," he said grabbing Aaron's hand in a friendly gesture, "but we need to explain a lot of things to you first."

Aaron looked up, frightened, straight into the brown eyes. He was afraid to hear a new type of truth, which was something different from the truth he had been aware of before.

"The cabin you have seen is the heart of the AS2. It is the Leader itself. It is a highly intelligent man-machine, a computer equipped with a human brain interface capable of thinking and making endless calculations."

Aaron pretended he did not hear anything. He pushed his bike forward without looking up.

"The AS2 is the abbreviation of the system, Atomic Strike 2. This base controls—with the other two islands—the counter-attack of the atomic war. We are all being trained how to survive the war situation..." Jack pointed around himself. His voice dropped away at the end and left some time for Aaron to digest the facts. But Aaron suddenly stopped and pushed his bike aside, shouting at Jack:

"I saw Dad! He was in that stasis-cabin, half naked. He looks like me and his face was the same as in the video-messages!" he shouted at the others.

"What you have seen was only a virtual image created by the *Leader*!" said Jack, catching Aarons flailing hands. "The *Leader* can appear in any form he wants! It can be your Dad, Mum, or your grandmother, or the *Leader*! For him it is only a way of communication and it makes things easier. It is nothing more."

"But he was there!" cried Aaron. "He pushed his hand to mine. His body was covered by wounds and scars from the interstellar war! He knew me and said I grew up so much!"

"Aaron," Jack shook him hard. "That was not your father! He is the *Leader*. It is a human machine created from one of your own brain cells. He only imitates being your father to motivate you to learn faster about the weapons. Don't you feel it, my dear soldier?"

Jack gasped intensively. He was also shocked that he had to tell the truth. He remembered clearly when his instructor told him the exact same truth on his eighteenth birthday. Jack let Aaron's hand slowly fall down next to his body when he stopped trying to fight.

"There is no interstellar war. There are no heroes, only us, the last deployable soldiers bred from human ovum and sperm. We are the human gears in a meaningless war-machine and—might be— the last survivors. Why do you think they took care of you so much?"

Aaron left them there with the bike. He did not care about his present anymore, because the bike was only a brick in the wall of lies.

"Hey mate," said Paul "don't leave it here. You can ride around on it a lot later, if we survive the coming days."

Aaron paid no attention anymore. *It was all lies*, he thought.

A bright headlight appeared in front of them on the road. It was Mr. Morton driving a four-wheeler.

"Welcome Mr. Spear and Mr. Paul and Kilian Breitner. I am happy that you safely disembarked on our island," said the humanoid robot after it stopped askew on the pass.

Aaron clambered to the back of the car as if Mr. Morton was not there. He looked apathetically through his instructor. The robot attached the bike to the car; he thought that the boy would like to use it one day after he calmed down. The Breitner brothers climbed next to Aaron, Jack sat in the right-front seat.

"What are the latest reports?" asked Jack, turning to Mr. Morton, who drove the car toward the base.

"I think they're preparing for a strike. This was the first sign. They've launched two intercontinental missiles with electromagnetic-blocking warheads to AS1 and 3. Only our air-defence could stop the rocket from reaching us. The electromagnetic waves blocked the power all over the island. They nullified even the emergency power of the droids. We just restored everything for now."

"What is the status of *Leader 1* and *3*?"

"Unfortunately, they have been destroyed. We have only *Leader 2* left. But we have a serious problem; Aaron did not reach the *level of weapons* yet, so he needs your professional help to control this last operable nuclear base. Aaron is a clever boy, but two weeks will not be enough to learn everything for the counterattack. We robots are not able to launch weapons. The launch protocol—written by the *Leader*—only accepts human orders."

Aaron did not say anything. He drew lines with the tip of his shoe into the dust.

"We can go through quickly in a threesome," said Jack turning back to the others. "If we're able to recover AS1 and 2 in the meantime, he can continue on his own."

Mr. Morton concentrated on the road.

"According to our intelligence, New-China has prepared for the final strike. Our home, the New-Hawaii-Island will not stay as it is now. The 4th World War is about to begin."

They rushed through the landscape. The door was not so far from them now.

"The most important thing in this delicate situation is your safety, as you are our potential survivors, soldiers, and responsible leaders," added Mr. Morton. "It will be beneficial for all of you to stay on the middle island. We have to concentrate on our task. When we go down to the AS2, we have to enter the scenarios suggested by *Leader 2* into the prediction system."

They floundered down from the car without words. Aaron did not show any interest in his bike; Paul helped him take it down the stairs.

"Master Aaron," Mr. Morton turned gently to the disillusioned boy. "I had no chance to wish you Happy Birthday due to the blackout. I would like to convey my best wishes in the name of Mrs. Elden too."

Aaron didn't even look at the robot.

The greatest birthday ever, he thought insensitively keeping his head down. *It might be my last one, knowing all circumstances.*

***

Mrs. Elden approached the middle of the sugarloaf temple, her rapping footsteps cut through the silence. She touched the cover of the sarcophagus. The pulsating blue light came to life, Mrs. Elden stepped back, waiting. One side of the tube became transparent and the face of a man—who called himself the Dad of Aaron—appeared in it.

"Good evening, Mrs. Elden."

"Good evening, *Leader*. Sorry to disturb you. I just wanted to ask you how the meeting was with Aaron. I came by in person; I did not want to use the internal communication lines."

"Hmm…" sighed the man, caressing his chin. "I really don't know. Perhaps I should not have done this to him, perhaps I should not deviate from the protocol. The most important thing of all is the counterattack. I should have waited for the first contact. The truth was too painful for him."

"Which truth?"

"The one he knows now. What the others might have told him."

The robot stayed in a long silence. She was hesitant to ask the question.

"What about the other truth, Mr. Sonnenfeld?"

"Which one, Mrs. Elden?"

"That we really did fight against aliens in the stars and you truly were injured in an interstellar battle; then we preserved your soul and kept it in this sarcophagus connected to the tactical computer."

The man remained silent. The cover of the tube became opaque again. Mrs. Elden patiently waited for a minute, and then she headed to the door. She had almost reached the handle when she heard the man's voice. He spoke weakly, just for himself.

"Why? Can it be a more painful truth in my situation than that I am the *Leader*?"

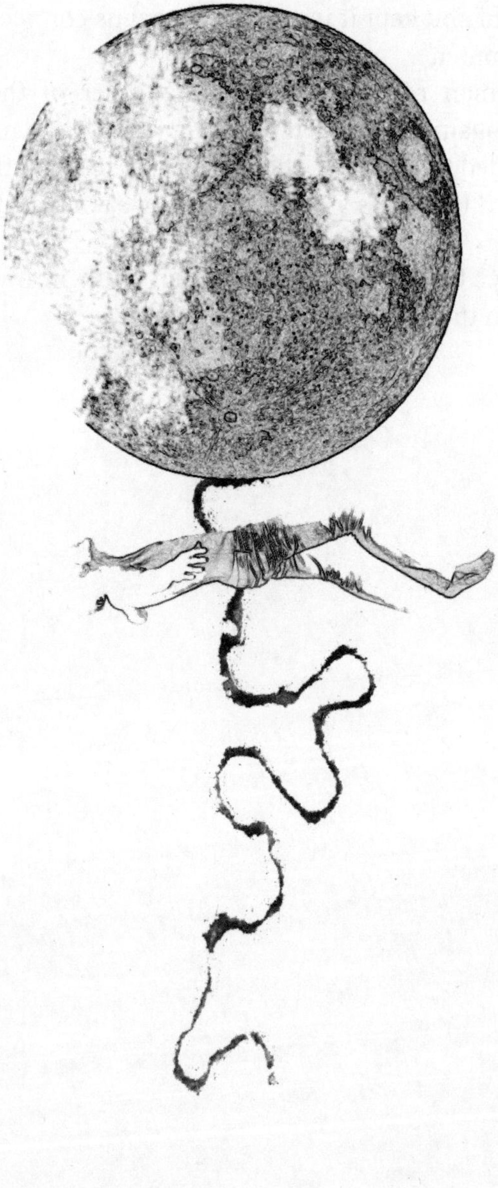

III.

Down on the River of Souls

—1—

Stephen Raymond Tapanazzi was the best in the business. He led the sales with more than twenty-two thousand successful contracts, and he'd scored these in the last five years alone. Others could not reach an average of ten thousand in ten years, but he surpassed those numbers within four years. He had received his promotional letter two weeks earlier, and now he sipped his coffee standing in his spacious, sunny office in the monumental Central Building, looking out over the view of the wealthy part of the city through gigantic glass panels.

The mighty mirroring windows of the neighboring skyscrapers reflected the purple colors of the clouds floating in the sunset. *As if Heaven would lie below my feet, bowing respectfully to me,* he thought. He saw himself on the pedestal when clouds of seventh heaven inclined before him. One final floor was above him: the office of the big boss. He had only one floor to climb to be the best.

The big boss had only done eighteen thousand sales when he took over the company. *He could have already been frightened to see the climbing agent below him,* Raymond thought. Raymond got three thousand sales more against the boss's extra floor. The gossip had already been circulating for months about the arrival of a new agent. The question was when would the first group of fawners arrive knocking on his door, holding *'Tapanazzi for Boss'* ballot papers in their hands? *If the time comes, I'll have to be very careful,* he thought.

He needed new friends; they would push him towards success.

As he stood above the world, an old song from his childhood popped into his head. His mother had shushed him with this little ditty, and he had no idea why it slipped into his mind at that moment. Maybe a fragrance or a mood triggered the switch of his brain to bring this song alive:

When the see-saw flies,
I sit on it with you,
You flew higher than the sky
Higher than the roof,
Up and down, up and down...

As he whistled, dreaming back to his childhood, Claire—his secretary, he'd got her the position—stood behind him. She smiled when Raymond turned to her.

"Oh, Claire, excuse my ill-breeding, I didn't hear you come in," said Raymond, embarrassed. He was still lost in his new position. The situation had changed a lot; he'd done everything by himself in the pokey, old office in Mission Bay, from paperwork to correspondence with the clients. Here, he had this magnificent, pretty creation of God—Claire—who dealt with all additional documentation tasks. Raymond could concentrate exclusively on sales.

"I apologize, Mr. Tapanazzi, I should have knocked much more loudly..."

She had a disarming smile, standing there in her flawless costume. Her shoulder-length, blonde hair was straightened, and her nametag was placed exactly five centimeters above her nipple, as described in the rules.

"... but you need to present yourself at the closing meeting," she added, sliding a large pile of documents onto the desk. She didn't seem to be a beginner; she must have worked with the previous record-holder. "The Director General, Mr. Pettyhorn, would like to see you, as his new Deputy Manager, before the meeting kicks off."

"He will be disappointed with me, because I am not as special as he might think," said Raymond, pretending modesty.

"Don't be too reserved, Mr. Tapanazzi. I was so eager to see the new record-holder who sold twenty-two thousand bodies in nearly five years!" She stood there, highlighting her blondness, pushing her left leg a little out to the side, which made her knee-length skirt stretch over her thigh. Raymond understood this body language very well, but he had no idea what he could do about it.

"Yes, you're right, surely I am the one," gestured Raymond with resignation, and stepped closer to his desk. "I admit that it was not easy to find clients for that number of bodies. A thousand hours of fieldwork had been invested in that success. And the paperwork!" He tapped the files standing on his desk like mountains.

"Then I'll leave you alone, as you only have two short hours to prepare for the meeting with Mr. Pettyhorn."

The door closed, and Tapanazzi was alone with the files. He would have to go through the company's latest sales. These statistics came from all around the world, not only from his old, little pothole. He was not just a county agent anymore: Raymond became one of four Deputy Directors at the company. And he was not only one of them, but *the* one: the record-holder. The best.

Either I'll cope with this task, fulfill the new post, or collapse, he thought.

*When the see-saw flies,
I sit on it with you,
. . .
Up and down, up and down . . .*

This old children's song: he crooned the catchy melody again and again. The sentences were so perfectly matched to his situation. He had to paddle intensively to keep his head above water.

Raymond rapidly opened the pile of documents and started the war with the statistics. *If it was working well in my little county, it will eventually work on a bigger scale,* he thought.

The coffee went cold on his desk, and the purple clouds turned to wild, dark whirls as the sun sank into the river valley.

—2—

The dredger took a wide turn towards the dam, as the captain wanted to avoid the huge concrete walls. He was a damn good sailor: only a few centimetres between his boat and the bank.
"Holy shit! This man knows his job, not like Harry at the chicken restaurant. If he parks your car, you're damned!" said Wilkins, the young sergeant, with a silly grin on his face. He

could be demeaning like a moron even if they worked on the hardest homicide case.

"My son, Wilkins, don't start now, please!" Lieutenant Greg Silverado reclined against the wall of the dam, watching the dredging. "I'm not in the mood for your bullshit right now. Run to the car and tell the captain that we're staying the whole night. It's going be a damned long night."

Wilkins ran up the riverside to the floating police car. The blue and red beams from the police lights colored the bare branches of the trees. It was a cold autumn evening.

This was the reason why Greg didn't want to come out of his warm office, but the dam operator's frightened voice had given him no choice; he had to come to the scene from Mission Bay Police Station. The *antigrav* police car flew here in thirty minutes. Of course, there was already a big audience; you can find priers everywhere, even in the shittiest pothole that Mission Bay was. The most interesting phenomenon was that they always outnumbered your expectations. The smaller the place, the bigger the crowd. Why? pondered Lieutenant Silverado, as he watched the smooth movement of the dredge. The excavated debris—sand and fist-sized gravel—had fallen to the bank from the long, heavy conveyor belt.

There were already six covered bodies lying ten metres from the debris. The heavy evening wind lifted the thick canvas from one. The amateur photographers from the crowd immediately made their *best-ever pictures*. Greg found it better to cover the body again; otherwise the news would be filled with the case. He couldn't stop the official press anyway, but he didn't want to serve the topic to the amateurs on a silver platter either.

The coroner's car stopped on the bank when it reached the bodies. With it came Phil Casey, one of his most experienced men.

"Hi, Greg." They shook hands. Phil was in his usual white coat and pair of rubber gloves. "What do you have for me?"

"Nothing special, Phil, we have some floaters. I don't know why—from where and why that many... but we may have more under the dam; the dredge is moving the sand floor near the wall at the moment."

"All right, but the dredge can damage them badly, especially if they aren't fresh."

"These are all fresh," said Greg, showing one of them. He tried to hide the sight from the photographers standing to the side. "They haven't been inflated or discoloured yet."

The coroner checked the other four. All of them were healthy-looking, young bodies. They were the naked corpses of four men and two women.

"These are all nudists or party-swimmers... but the weather is too cold for that," said the doctor. "Their deaths could have happened only a few hours earlier. Didn't you find clothes?"

"No. The dam operator found them. They emerged near the wall here. He said they came up every five minutes. It's an interesting case, like a collective suicide." Silverado shook his head. He'd been in this field a long, long time but had never seen such a thing before.

Wilkins came back from the car. "The captain says he will make every effort to get out of his bed and will be here in fifteen minutes. He wants to see everything."

The Lieutenant looked meaningfully at the doctor.

"Then we don't sleep tonight," he added peevishly.

"Here! Come here!" shouted the dam operator. He stood next to the conveyor belt. "We've found more!"

They covered the bodies, and Wilkins placed some rocks at the edge of the canvas. Lieutenant Silverado and the coroner arrived at the operator, who looked very sick, covering his mouth with his hand. He pointed to the ground. "These are in a much worse condition than the others."

The four bodies didn't look nice at all. The dredger had crushed them hard; their limbs were scrambled into a mess. The coroner crouched to check them.

"It is interesting that these have been dead for much longer than the others. I estimate they were underwater nearly two weeks."

"And they're old, or middle-aged. Those are all young," said Silverado, puzzled. "This is not a nudist swimming course at all."

"Oh, God, another two—" said the operator, devastated. He turned his back on the sight in severe disgust. The conveyor belt was filled with twisted body parts. After a short trip, they dropped down at the end of the belt and slid to the foot of the officials.

"They're all the same," said the coroner.

"For God's sake!" Greg swore. "How long will it take to get anything out of this?"

The coroner's eyes stayed cloudy: there was no sign of optimism in them. "I might have some results tomorrow, or definitely after tomorrow. In two days I'll finish these twelve, if there are no more."

They looked careworn towards the water where the dredger went for another long turn. Meanwhile, the conveyor belt just brought all the squalor of the river to their feet.

— 3 —

Pettyhorn looked totally different from the pictures Raymond had seen of him. In those portraits he was twenty years younger. It looked as if they didn't refresh those pictures on purpose; the big boss—as the Managing Director of the emerging and energetic new cloning company, The Young Body for the Future—did not want to be an elderly man. But, in reality, he was.

"Stephen R. Tapanazzi! The record-holder himself! And he is with me in the Central Office, only working for me from now on!" said Pettyhorn, passing by his desk. He was shorter than Raymond by a head. "After the zillions of stories I've heard about you, I feel like I've already known you for ages!"

"I hope all those stories had happy endings, Mr. Director," said Raymond, facilely. He wanted to radiate the laxness he used to enthral his colleagues. In communication he was unbeatable.

Raymond could observe the real Pettyhorn without euphemistic retouching. He was said to be seventy; his prominent cheekbones made him look a little aggressive. His face resembled his reputation: many agents were afraid of him. He fired many of Raymond's colleagues without qualms if they did not deliver the monthly quota. His lean hand made the handshake painful. Rumors said that it was already a good sign if he shook somebody's hand.

"Have a seat!" Pettyhorn showed him to the luxury leather armchair. "If you paddle that quickly, you'll soon be on this side of the desk!"

He is starting to be sarcastic, thought Raymond. *He's afraid of me. He knows that a new lobby group—formed by some powerful opponent shareholders—could push him right off his throne. They'd already done that with Pettyhorn a few years ago, when* he reached his new record of eighteen thousand sales. The wings of luck picked him up, and the previous record-holder had to leave. Although that wasn't enough to be a record-holder: you needed to have influential sponsors. Raymond's name was not strong enough at the moment... but it might be in a few years.

"Oh, no, I'm not that dangerous. I owe my success mostly to lucky contracts," said Raymond, trying to feign modesty again. This might be the best weapon against Pettyhorn.

"Come on, Tapanazzi, you know something valuable," waved the director. "I don't believe that you only had luck to get into those prisons and nursing homes. You had to have talent for that. You must have a good business sense, persuasive skills, and an excellent financial background. Don't forget: you're speaking with the former record-holder. I know everything inside out!" said Pettyhorn, sitting up proudly.

"So, forget all courtesy. I'm more than happy that you're the new strong man in our international team!" added Pettyhorn with a prim smile, and he turned to the projector wall. A huge hologram came out of it.

"Here you can see our growing empire around the world. According to your capabilities, you will have the responsibilities of two new markets—East and South Africa. Don't be frightened." He smiled ironically at Raymond, the smile of a jealous rival. "You'll handle them easily. These are rising, valuable markets with four to five thousand estimated sales per year. It will be a refreshing experience after the quiescent business of the Midwest."

"I have exactly the same view about it," lied Raymond. He knew he would have struggles. He had left the road where everything and everybody was familiar, well-known, and stuffed with black money. There would be no payoff, established connections; he would have to start everything from scratch. But he had already accepted this position, so there was no way back. County or continent, it was almost the same. The second was maybe a bigger challenge . . .

"And it will be a great opportunity for you to know more about the developments of our company," finished Pettyhorn. Raymond was embarrassed; he hoped that the boss didn't notice that he was deeply immersed in his own thoughts.

"I'm delighted to know more about the new developments: I'm an innovative person myself," he lied again. He didn't care about the developments at all; he was only interested in how he could increase his sales and his payslip.

"Then let me introduce our new product to you," said Pettyhorn with a theatrical gesture, opening a gap between two walls. There was an engagingly beautiful, ebony-skinned women standing in the space.

"Oh, you said '*product*'?" smiled Raymond, amazed.

"You're surprised, aren't you?" Pettyhorn was totally ecstatic at the view. "I would like to introduce Sheba to you. She is the new cyber-biodroid of the company, powered by a human brain. She's our winning new card in the market."

Sheba was standing there with a prescriptive, wide smile and strikingly bright teeth. In the blue costume of the company—knee-length shirt and jacket—she looked like the ancient Queen of Sheba.

"Nice to meet you," said Raymond, hesitating as to which form of welcome would be appropriate for a cyborg. She was not entirely a human or a clone.

"I am also pleased to meet you, sir," she said, keeping the same perfect smile. The only part of her body that moved was her nicely shaped lips. "May I have your name, please?"

"Of course, Sheba. My name is Stephen Raymond Tapanazzi, I am the new Deputy Director of the company."

"I welcome you, Mr. Stephen Raymond Tapanazzi. It is good to know you, sir."

There is something strange about this woman, Raymond thought. Her smile and her body were like a human fashion model, but she carried the weakness of a new model, too.

"So what do you think, Tapanazzi?" Pettyhorn was over-the-top excited. "She is the first prototype. Ebony."

"Perfect body, exclusive manners. She'll be the hit product against the Betty-blue droids." Raymond referred to the Paris doll-looking cyborg of their competitors, which had been released the previous year.

"That's it, Tapanazzi, you said exactly the truth. And why is she coloured ebony?"

Raymond looked perplexed. He wanted to say that there was no other type of skin in the clone-lab at the moment.

"Because she's your personal cyborg assistant! She will go with you to Africa!"

Tapanazzi was not totally enthusiastic, but he didn't want to disappoint the big boss, so he nodded with appreciation and a big smile on his face.

Sheba did not move at all. There was something creepy in the way she was standing in the moonlight, looking at Raymond. Something artificially creepy.

It was very late. Raymond would have to get used to the night meetings that the Board of Directors here liked so much. *It's going to be a very long night*, he thought.

— 4 —

Phil, the coroner of the Mission Bay Police Department, found some explanations much easier than he expected. Those microchips implanted in the arms of the bodies helped him a lot.

The young group looked like they were just past their thirties, but according to their data they were all over sixty. One of them—a woman—was eighty years old. Three had just been released from the local prison—two of them were burglars, and one was a white-collar criminal. The old woman was a member of the pensioners' home in Mission Bay, although her body was as fresh as that of a budding teenager.

Phil reviewed the identification of the chips; they were all issued by The Young Body for the Future Corporation, which meant that they were all clones. All of them were naked, with no signs of external or internal physical damage. Their lungs were filled with water after their deaths, but it was very hard to determine this in the case of clones. The rapidly developing clone technology was modifying the structure of human cells to make them live much longer than natural cells. He had to find the exact model number to determine the accurate time of death.

The other—older—six were totally different. All of them were heavily decayed. In the worst condition was the oldest woman. The cause of death: heart failure, in all six cases. Somebody released the blood from their bodies by cutting their arteries. It had happened a few weeks before.

They finally could identify the six pairs: each pair composed of a body of the owner and his rented clone. Phil did not understand how it could have happened; as he knew this technology, the owner—and user—of the clone had to stay under stasis while his soul was implanted in the rented or owned clone body. They could not both be out at the same time.

But this was not his problem anymore. He had given the case to Lieutenant Silverado.

"Look, Jack, it's evident. This guy is a shifty agent, he sells clone bodies. According to the registrations, he sold all of those we just found. He is a sales record-holder, he rose straight through the ranks to Deputy Director."

Captain Jack Borrows was listening to Greg as they watched the young, well-dressed agent on the monitor. The young man had sweat through his ironed white shirt in circular patches. They had lifted him from the night directorial board meeting.

"He generated his record sales through unclean and unlawful means. All his clients were from prisons and pensioners' homes," added Silverado meaningfully, winking at the captain. "These are not the top-selling places for these bodies . . ."

"Not really," the captain shook his head. He wore a black cowboy hat; the water was still dripping from its brim. "But we'll find out why he was so successful in those . . ." he stopped mid-sentence. "What is he singing?"

"It's an old little ditty about a see-saw. He doesn't seem to be frightened; I'm sure he's just trying to fool us. He thinks he did everything by the books."

"All right," sighed the captain. "Show him the evidence and put some pressure on him. But be careful, not too quickly. You have the winning card."

"No question, Jack." Greg patted the thick, artificial bear-fur coat on his boss's shoulder. "Trust me."

He took the pile of photos from the table and left the room.

—5—

Raymond's stomach was upset by the smell of coffee. The previous evening had started with a nice cup of coffee in his new office—and finished with another type of coffee. And he didn't want to taste that one.

He twisted and turned his jacket—though it wasn't cheap material it was looking as worn as he was—like soaked hemp rope.

There was only a digital clock on the wall of the interrogation room; the red numbers resembled vertical and horizontal lines beamed through the half-light.

Suddenly a man stepped into the room, the same one he'd seen in the corridor before—he looked important, a high-ranking officer, always on his communicator. *He must have the red ace*, Raymond thought.

"Mr. Tapanazzi, I am Lieutenant Greg Silverado, I'm leading the investigation in your case."

He wore a quilted, padded vest above his jacket. Raymond could see the handle of his weapon under his arm. Only a quick, sudden jump and he could have it...

"I think if I stay silent, you'll tell me without pressure what we should know about this story."

Raymond's mind was still on the gun, *I won't be that quick*, though, *and it would make this situation even crazier*. "What should I say?" asked Raymond as he stopped twisting his jacket momentarily. He unfolded it, trying to get the original shape back, but it was soaked with sweat.

"Don't you know?" The stocky policeman turned theatrically to the cameras, spreading his arms wide. Raymond was sure he was acting to somebody on the other side of the observance room.

"What? The officer who brought me in accused me of multiple homicide and destruction of clone bodies. They mentioned my rights, nothing more. I couldn't call my lawyer."

"Right, Mr. Tapanazzi, soon you'll get a minute to call your lawyer, but until then we can have a chat. Just the two of us," the policeman winked reassuringly.

He is a bumpkin, thought Raymond. *Why should I speak without a lawyer?*

"What are you offering? What will I gain from a private conversation?"

Silverado's eyes brightened.

"I can't offer more than the law gives you: mitigating circumstances if you give a testimony."

Raymond was counting on a more generous offer, like they'd let him go home. He didn't commit those crimes they mentioned. He wasn't always clear with the business, but that was something else.

"So, do you want to hear that I made my record by killing people?"

"Yes, exactly," said Silverado firmly. He felt himself already winning and leaned on the table with the gesture of a merciful king. He played again to his superior.

"There's only one slight problem, Lieutenant Silverado: I did not kill anybody. I admit, I wasn't always on the narrow path of the law, but I did not kill anybody."

Silverado jumped from the table and threw photos in front of Raymond.

"And these? These are bodies of clones and their owners. We just fished them out of the Mission River. Do you know what the press calls our beloved river?" Small drops of saliva flew from his mouth as he shouted insanely. "*The river of souls*, for God's sake. This is the new name of our magnificent river because people like you float dead bodies in it!"

"That wasn't part of my business strategy," answered Raymond. "The dead tenant is not a good tenant for one very good reason—they cannot pay anymore for the clone bodies."

Silverado calmed down and sat back next to the table.

"I understand," he said. "Then please tell me more about the system. Convince me that you had no interest in killing those people."

"How can I do that? You came with the preconception that I'm a killer."

"Try it!" Silverado made the same irritating pose for the cameras.

He is a true rural buffoon, thought Raymond.

"Right," agreed Raymond. He felt for the first time that he could compose his thoughts. He took a sip of that hated, cold, horrible coffee. "I've been employed by The Young Body for the Future for four years already. I began work at the County Center as an agent, and I felt I was superb. Then I attracted the Central Office with my work, so they started to sponsor me."

"What exactly does that mean?"

"They monitored and helped my sales. I felt weird about this close attention, but I finally got used to it. I thought it was a way of supporting talented people here. Then the scheduled promotion came."

"You were promoted to Head of Regional Office."

"Exactly. And from that moment, my sales went ballistic."

"What was different from before?"

"I got my orders from Head Office. They determined which segment of the market I needed to aim at," answered Raymond. *It doesn't matter anymore*, he thought, *I'll tell the whole story. I really don't want to be arrested.*

"You started to get clients from prisons and pensioners' homes," said Silverado, sliding two contracts to Raymond.

They were quick, thought Raymond. *They got the papers in two hours.*

"Yes, I did." There was no way back anymore, he would have to continue. He took a long sip from the sticky black liquid they called coffee here.

"Can you explain to me the process of the clone rental? What do I need to do to have a clone body?"

"It's dead easy. One of my colleagues will contact you and ask about your motivation: why you want to rent a clone body. Then we check if we have a *suitable* subject for you in the warehouse. We have more than four hundred thousand bodies at the moment."

"What does suitable mean?" asked Silverado, surprised.

"We have to condition the clone body for your personality: let me say, for your soul. This isn't always a successful procedure. You cannot have the body if the conditioning is not successful. If we do the body switch despite an unsuccessful conditioning, we can lose your soul in the process. You will disappear, dissolve in this very sensitive phase. Your memories will not be transferred totally into the new body, so your clone will only partially be you. Everything would have to be learned again."

"I understand," said the lieutenant. He breathed heavily and noisily. He definitely would have needed a young clone body. "If the conditioning is successful, what is the next step?"

"Then you come to the Regional Center and sit in the stasis cabin. From this moment your rental is active."

"And what happens with my body in stasis?"

"Nothing at all. Your body is dead without your soul. We keep the vegetative function up and store your body until the rent is over."

"What happens if the clone dies in an accident with the owner's soul inside?" asked Silverado, playing with a cartridge case and beating a discontinuous rhythm on the surface of the table.

"Then the owner's soul will be lost totally. The original body in stasis will be useless. The insurance company will pay for the clone body. Otherwise they're really valuable pieces; we breed them for as long as the normal child grows up."

"Pieces—" Silverado's face radiated indignation. "You strangely call a human body born from human cells 'pieces.'"

"This is my job," answered Raymond to the provocative sentence. He looked at the rings made by the coffee cup on the shiny surface of the table without any emotion. "You deal with dead bodies, too. The clone bodies are not living creatures before the client rents them. They're just objects in stasis."

"Isn't that unethical?"

"Mr. Silverado, if our government accepted the law of clone commerce, why wouldn't I?" Raymond knew that he'd always followed the law. They couldn't catch him from that side.

"Yes, you're right. Forget it. It's just my personal moral problem. Tell me more about the sales you did in the prisons and pensioners' homes. How can you make contracts there? They're not the type of people who can afford a clone body."

"I told you: the company sponsored me. They gave financial aid after the first ten thousand sold."

"How did they do that?"

"They gave names of who I needed to contact about the contracts. Of course, nobody let me into these places just as a favor. The contracted clients got huge discounts."

"So all other regular agents sold at the registered price, except you. Didn't you think there was something suspicious about that?"

Raymond had always suspected there was something fishy behind the scenes. But he concentrated only on the sales statistics.

"No," he lied. "I didn't care about this whole thing. I thought there were some powerful lobbyists behind the money and the support I received who wanted to displace the big boss. I thought they wanted to put me in his place."

The lieutenant took the ten pictures and arranged them into five pairs.

"I'm ready to believe you if you can explain to me why you called these clone-users back for a coordination meeting two weeks before you were promoted." Silverado put some papers on the table with written phone conversations tapped by the intelligence service. "You told them they had to come into the center for data reconciliation."

"I had to do that. This is the handover procedure. I had to call in all users—I did it with the other two hundred bodies—whose contracts will be finished in the changing period, to give a clean sheet to my successor."

"I understand. And what happened in these meetings?"

"Nothing in particular," answered Raymond. "I just told them I was leaving them, and if they wanted to have their original bodies back, they could have them. Two of my old clients used this option."

The policeman took his communicator and turned to Raymond. There was video footage from a surveillance camera on it.

"This footage is from the Regional Office at Mission Bay. You can see five clones arriving at the time you fixed the rendezvous with them. Look. They arrived there... but none of them left the building. That's you, very late at night, when you left the office. But nobody else. Neither the clone owners, nor the clones..."

"That's absolutely normal," explained Raymond. "We need to condition each body for a night. We transfer their personalities back into the original bodies. These five had their mandatory conditioning procedure on that day. You can watch the footage of the next day, you'll see them leaving."

The lieutenant looked deeply into Raymond's eyes.

"From this moment there was no more footage recorded, Mr. Tapanazzi. Don't you find that interesting?"

Raymond found it more frightening than interesting. "How can that be? My successor didn't record anymore?"

"No. It's more bizarre than that: you didn't have a successor at all."

"What? I spoke with him on the phone," said Raymond, astonished. He shook his head and got a swirling feeling in his stomach.

"But you've never seen him, have you?"

Silverado was right. They had never met. His successor always had a busy schedule.

"His name is Hugh Bloomington. He's got engaging manners. I thought he would be the perfect salesman."

"Strange, but there is no employee with this name registered at your company."

Raymond guessed this answer.

"Mr. Tapanazzi, I just received the report right before I came into this room that the building of your company, The Young Body for the Future, in Mission Bay, has been set on fire and colleagues from the Fire Department fought to save it. Unfortunately, they could not save the stasis cabins and the owner's original bodies. Exactly 22,362 human bodies have vanished in the fire—according to the stock numbers we got from Head Office."

"What?" Raymond couldn't believe what he was hearing. The last twenty-four hours were turning into a complete nightmare.

"Then all the users stuck in their clone bodies won't be able to find hosts for the time of conditioning. This is impossible! Where will we get so many available bodies from?"

Lieutenant Silverado had reached the end of his one-man show. He felt that Tapanazzi had broken already, that this was the time to tighten the rope around his neck, although with all the evidence he didn't see the agent being guilty of arson.

"Look, I know I can't lock you up for starting a fire, but I'm not sure that you are innocent about the bodies floating in the river. I have to show you this upsetting photo. This could be the one that exempts you from prosecution. I don't believe that you could do this just for the money."

He slid his last piece of evidence onto the table. Tapanazzi's eyes flooded with tears as he picked up the picture. It had his mother's barely recognizable face on it.

"Oh, my mother . . ." A tear rolled down his face. "My successor talked me into bringing her into the sponsored program. She lived in the Mission Bay Pensioners' Home. I hope you don't think I could . . ."

"I don't know what I should think." Silverado stood up. "Your—and your lawyer's—task is to prove your innocence in front of the court. I will order an investigation into the Head Office of The Young Body for the Future Corporation. I have to keep you inside until my colleagues collect all the evidence."

The door closed silently after the policeman.

Stephen Raymond Tapanazzi had only his little ditty in his ear, echoing his mother's voice, while his tears fell onto the photo:

When the see-saw flies,
I sit on it with you,
. . .

—6—

There was a huge crowd at the press conference. Story-hungry correspondents fired with their photo cameras or controlled their floating robot cameras towards the podium. The Board of Directors of The Young Body for the Future Corporation was represented at the long desk.

"Ladies and gentlemen, may I ask for a little attention? I promise I will answer all your questions soon, but first I have to explain what really happened last night. I have a small surprise waiting for you afterwards," started Director General Pettyhorn.

The reporters fell silent.

"First of all, some words about the regrettable events of last night. We have appointed a new Deputy Director who reached the record sales of twenty-two thousand!"

A murmur waved through the crowd on hearing the record high number.

"I am not able to introduce this person to you, because he's in jail for the moment. The police investigation has found evidence that he raised his sales by unfair means. They've fished out twelve bodies from the Mission River, already being called *'the river of souls'*. All bodies are registered under the name of Stephen Raymond Tapanazzi, the previously mentioned, greatly anticipated new Deputy Director, who made his contracts in prisons and pensioners' homes by blackmailing the managers of these establishments."

Another big rumble broke out from the listeners.

"Yes, ladies and gentlemen, this is a big shame for the company. He set fire—with his accomplice, Hugh Bloomington—to the Regional Office of our company building in Mission Bay in order to hide their tracks. All bodies—the owners and the clones on stock—were destroyed in the flames. You can see how diabolical this plan was, with the clear motivation to acquire my directorial chair."

He couldn't stop the outbreak of questions coming from the other side.

"Yes, I will answer all questions." He raised his hand to calm everybody down. "But first I want you to have a great experience, not to finish the day with bad memories." He circled the long table and gestured theatrically to a curtain sliding away. A big bright beam of light appeared on the emerging clear white canvas. The hall darkened, and the people stopped speaking.

"Let me introduce to you the newest epoch-making invention of The Young Body for the Future Corporation, which will make you forget all the bad episodes of last night. Our new star, the model that is more long-standing and magnificent than the clones, the cyborg, which works with a human soul: the Queen of Sheba!"

A beautifully rocking woman's body came into the middle of the spotlight. She walked to the edge of the pulpit then took up a model's position, placing her leg nicely to the side. A silver swimsuit stretched over her ebony skin.

The crowd erupted into applause and whistles.

Pettyhorn had aimed for exactly this. He wanted to divert attention away from what had happened last night. And his plan was successful.

In a few days, they would start production. They got an order for exactly 22,362 new models.

"Please, sing something! We want to hear if her voice is as beautiful as her body!" asked someone from the crowd, but Pettyhorn intervened.

"I'm so sorry, you have to understand that the soul of the cyborg is in the learning phase now. Not all your questions are self-evident to her. We can look for an old song in the memory of the donor's soul, if there is any. The brain might have kept something after the conditioning process."

He gently caressed the cyborg.

"Sheba, can you sing something to our audience?"

Sheba had been standing in the same feminine position from the moment she stood at the pulpit, and smiled as if she were in thought. She slowly turned to Pettyhorn then back to the reporters. Someone hissed for silence.

The wonderful voice of the ebony cyborg filled the hall as she sang:

When the see-saw flies,
I sit on it with you,
You flew higher than the sky
Higher than the roof,
Up and down, up and down . . .

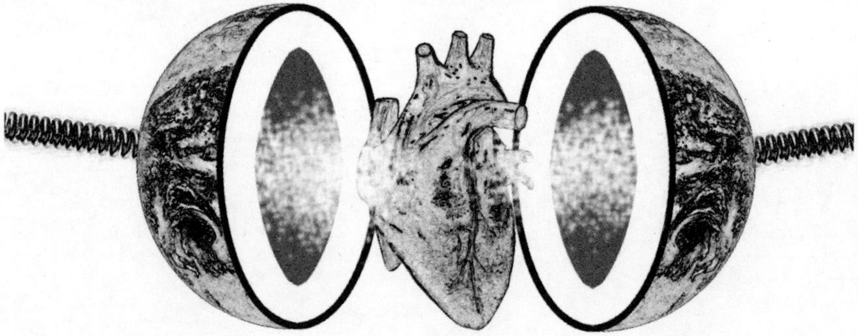

IV.

The Reanimator

"Why did you reanimate him?"

The echoing question bounced back and forth in Joshua's head, and he had no idea where it came from and how long it would stay. But it did stay—the whole morning.

It was very hard to wake up, every part of his body was in pain. The persistent pulsation deep in his bones had not been allowed to sleep for many years. This unbearable pain cut a wide obsessive gap in his days into which all the important and beautiful part of his life fell.
Only the enveloping, milky fog, coming with the pain, stayed with him.

He had to wake up; but his bed pulled him back. The massage extension—built into the mattress—helped him a lot. He could enjoy that for hours. But the day had to be started like all other days before.

It was not easy to find his slippers. He couldn't imagine how they'd gone so far from the bed, although he always took them off in the same way: he sat down on the edge of the bed and simply slipped out of them. If they did not come off easily, they could slide a maximum of three centimetres to the side or forward. But not three and a half metres from the bed, as they were this morning. They had wandered up to the dining table.

Buster, the old shepherd dog, came into his mind—was it Buster, or Scruffy? Or was Scruffy before Buster? He couldn't remember clearly anymore. Good old Buster! He used to take one of the slippers, and when Joshua scolded him he would bring it back . . . but not the slipper, the newspaper!

It was awfully long ago! How long was it? He had reanimated Buster three times, and lost him at the end when his heart could not cope with the interventions. That was only a prototype of the present *Reanimator* model, he'd had to fine-tune it for years. He touched the spot just below the lump on his sternum—it was there, operating. Although it might be time to get rid of it forever. . . .

He shuffled towards his slippers. One of them was below the table—he inched it out with his walking stick. It surely was an earthquake, otherwise it could not have flown that far from the bed. Everything was tied down in the kitchen and on the table, thus he could only hear faint clinks in the event of an earthquake. Sometimes he didn't even wake up for that.

Like this time. Had he slept through it again? How could that be? He slept so uneasily, so little. . . .

He opened the curtains and expected to see chaos and devastation, but it was all silent and peaceful out there. The hospital and the surroundings were intact; no whiffs of smoke, no running survivors or crowds on the street like long ago when half the city had been destroyed.

This could have been a small, localized earthquake. He might have slept through it as he had done on other occasions.

"Why did you reanimate him?"

He heard the sentence again, completely clearly, as if somebody was speaking in his head. This voice scared him to death; he had never had hallucinations. Would senility start like this?

They knew him as a man of knowledge and wisdom, as an honoured scientist. He had never had to fight against psychological problems; he'd never used drugs or other unlawful substances to make himself relaxed or even numb—he hated that state. Otherwise, how could he be the genius of human life prolongation? He had a creed—*we can search for the ultimate wisdom only with a clear consciousness.*

Maybe the television would help to cast that materialized thought out of his head. As he looked up, the TV set stood askew on the shelf. In fact, the shelf was skewed and the box had slipped to the corner. It had smashed the vase: all the shards were lying on the floor along the wall. The orphaned artificial flower—*had Irene brought them?*—was stuck between the plastic and the wood, shouting for help. He poked it with his walking stick, and the silk rose spun twice before landing on the floor. *Somebody will help lift it*, he thought. He didn't dare bend to get it. He didn't have good balance anymore, not even to walk.

Strictly speaking, he didn't walk much anymore. The maximum distance was to the dining table. Who knows when he was last in the kitchen? The cutlery and plates would stay clean for eternity. He didn't understand why the room was furnished with this expensive kitchen equipment if he had never needed it—he got all his food through tubes.

The whole ritual to wake up and stand was only done by rote. Most of the time he put on his slippers, stood up, and then sat back.

Yes, it was true that he floundered to the window especially after the earthquake. Every two months he went there even if there was no trembling, just to see the houses, traffic, movements. To see some trace of life around him.

When was the last time Irene had come? It must have been twenty or even twenty-five years since he'd last seen his daughter. He couldn't remember if she brought that silk rose or if it had just been sent. The details of his personal life got blurred in his mind, as if all the data slid deeper and deeper between two drawers of his mind-folder with every quake.

Sometimes he lost consciousness in the case of a tremor. It could even be that he died once or twice. He could not tell the difference between fainting and death. Both were the same regarding consciousness, and both of them finished with waking up, thanks to the *Reanimator*.

"*Why did you reanimate him?*"

What was this? Or who was this?

He was not frightened anymore, as the voice was already familiar. There was no sign of malice—he could even hear incomprehension and curiosity. It sounded like the nice and not interrogative voice of a mature man. He was friendly. It could be somebody from the past—from that past, which had slid between the two drawers of his mind-folder.

Oh yes, the TV, he thought. He'd forgotten about it again. It would help him to get back to a rhythm.

He pushed the button on the remote, but the screen was full of white noise. The antenna cable might be detached or have become loose. There was some recognizable movement in the background. It was good that he had not floundered back to his bed, so he could push the cable with his walking stick. The picture suddenly cleared.

"The scientists registered an earthquake of seven magnitudes all over the globe today," said the reporter. Joshua could see the reporter's Eastern features and well-manicured, red nails as she held the paper in front of her. *When was the last time I could cut my own nails?* he thought.

"It is not known why the tremors are more frequent and higher in magnitude, but one thing is sure: we need to do something in order to protect the population," the woman continued.

I've seen this situation, pondered Joshua. It looked like everything was repeating. It was the same woman saying the same words "in order to protect the population." But what could she say in the case of a catastrophe? She could say something like "for the safety of humankind...."

"Why did you reanimate him?"

"No! She can't say that! Get out of my head!" Joshua was shocked by his own voice. In truth, he hadn't had a chance to speak with anybody for a long time. Irene had not called him for twenty years. She was his only daughter, but their relationship had become empty and cold. It was due to the death of Joshua's wife, who had tested the first prototype of the *Reanimator* with him. Irene would never forgive him for using her mother in the experiments.

Bad, bad past! It would never go away, reanimated with us each time we started again with all our mistakes and disappointments. *Damned piece of junk, go to Hell!*—he smashed at the small bump on his chest as much as he could. He held in his breath for a moment, but the *Reanimator* quickly corrected the situation; it relaxed the cramped muscles and helped to start the lungs again with small electric shocks.

"It is hard to predict when the next hit will come," said the expert sitting in the studio. "In any case, I suggest staying inside buildings: all structures made *fully* earthquake-resistant."

"Fully," repeated Joshua mechanically. It was good to hear his voice through his eardrums, not just to listen to the inner ones. The expert spoke the truth; the last big earthquake—which almost ruined his room—could have been a hundred or a hundred and fifty years ago. There were no big ones after that, just small ones like last night.

"It was a huge mistake."

He wanted to throw his stick at the safety window when he heard the voice again, but he changed his mind. The thin aluminium stick could not go that far.

Well, the voice—or the guy in his head—wanted to say something else as well. It sounded firmly sad when he pronounced those two words. It sounded like self-accusation had spoken to him. Might be that unspoiled person he had been long ago. . . .

Yes, he had weaknesses, a lot of them! He was most ashamed of his selfishness. The egoism had advanced his career and controlled his decisions.

The interests of humankind above all! Eternity is a social need!—he had said in many interviews justifying his experiment. The people wanted more than a hundred and thirty years, they wanted to live two hundred or more! Why not? Demand is the biggest motivation in the scientific world.

"For those selfish careerists, like you," Shearer, his co-researcher, had said. He'd disagreed with the strategy of selling out science only for money. "Maybe for others; but for us, science is something more sublime."

Yes, you say this, you were the military's bright star shooting the nerve-blocking weapons into success, Joshua thought with an ironic smile. His lips stretched over his toothless gums for a moment, then the grimace disappeared together with the aching thoughts. It was long ago . . .

". . . overpopulation is a huge problem in addition to the quakes—the cause of this goes back three centuries." He caught half-sentences from the expert's speech as the TV brought him back to the present.

Yes, it was nearly three hundred years ago when the Eternal Life Society started to finance his studies. The founders of the Society were the owners of the biggest companies searching for interplanetary energy sources, so a long life was a professional criterion for them. The pilots were worth a great deal if they survived the hundred and fifty years of long missions. Not just simply survived, but maintained in complete sanity and strength when they came home.

They tested the second-generation *Reanimators*. This small device prolonged the genetically modified age by a hundred years or more. The aging sped up in the human body after the age of a hundred and fifty. People had to go through operations to implant organs and bones after long years charging their skeletons and muscles. The *Reanimator* helped them in these crisis situations; on the interplanetary journeys they did not have complete medical teams for a heart transplant, even if they had enough cloned hearts. The Eternal Life Society grasped onto Joshua's product.

"One day or another doesn't mean anything."

The voice didn't bring him out of past memories, because he thought about those malicious attacks he'd had to go through. The scientific world excommunicated him.

"One day or another for a hundred-and-sixty-year-old does not count at all," they said. "Why did you change the order of nature? Didn't we do enough harm to push our limits to the maximum? What do we do with the elderly?"

". . . it's certainly caused by congestion. The carrying capacity of the present population is decreasing more and more, which leads to inevitable tensions and maybe war," said the expert on the TV. "The earthquakes became bigger after the Third World War, when the axis of the Earth was angled seven degrees more by the explosions of atomic warheads. This was followed by the slipping of the magnetic poles, which increased tectonic movements and generated earthquakes of a higher magnitude."

"You're damned wrong, my friend," murmured Joshua to the speaker. The slide—or even switch—of magnetic poles would not lead to an earthquake; these were legends in light of the latest geological evidence. The magnetic field would not vanish—it could happen that we would have more than one North and South Pole. A change in the Earth's axis could cause climatic change, but not earthquakes!

How can you come out all the time with the same fabulous and unscientific story? he thought. *And you call me an outlaw. . . .*

He calmed down slowly.

This damned TV brought out the past all the time and confronted him with the reality that came from these spoiled events. Why didn't he just watch a nice movie? Why did he always need to irritate himself with pseudo-scientific speculations? Why didn't he just remember his personal memories?

Because they were as bad as the professional ones. . . .

"However painful to admit."

The mystical traveller in his head had been right; Joshua nodded. It was so painful to admit that he was irresponsible, heartless, and unable to show love.

"Because you always ignored her," Irene had shouted, at the party after her mother's funeral. "When she didn't want to live anymore, you still didn't care! What kind of life did she have with you? When did you spend an intimate day with her? Not a day . . . just one hour, only the two of you! You bonded her to yourself when she was terminally ill. Your damn Reanimator just pumped the life into her while she was still suffering!"

"Mea culpa . . ." said Joshua loudly. He wanted to fall on his knees, but he couldn't stand up and he couldn't reach the emergency button. Then he would have to wait until somebody noticed that he was in trouble. Was it worth begging for forgiveness like this? If nobody could see it?

"You were always interested in externality," he heard Irene's voice from the past again. "Professor God, they called you around the world. The Big Magician!"

She was right. He loved the limelight and the world praised him as the saviour of mankind. Joshua trained the new generation of *Reanimators*—agents hired by the Eternal Life Society—who preached of luxurious long life. The Society benefitted greatly from the invention but ruined the world at the same time. People called them false prophets.

The *Reanimator* circled the world on a successful tour. At the same time, the world had sunk into a deep economic depression. Everybody financed his eternal life, the wonder-gadget, from loans. The aging population could not sustain itself; the unemployment rate shot sky-high. That was the time when the Third World War started.

"You don't even deserve that I put you in hospital," said Irene, during her farewell. Joshua turned one hundred and sixty-six that year. Of course, Irene didn't want to have the *Reanimator* implanted. . . .

Yes, Joshua remembered finally, *she couldn't bring the silk rose because she died nearly a hundred and sixty years ago.*

That rose was from her grave.

"This is cruelty!"

He agreed with the mystical stranger living in his head. The cruelty was when a parent buried his child. This shouldn't have happened.

What was the sense taking over God's place? To gain a few years, a few days? What for, if everything was just falling through the thief's fingers like golden sand?

Wars, crises, greed, and families falling apart—a man-made cataclysm.

"Where are you now, God?" When he asked the question, a huge shock pushed him down from the bed. He shouted loudly while he flew towards the dining table. His slippers slid beside the walls. There was no question now how they wandered so far from the bed last night. The shelf couldn't survive; it had fallen down towards the slippers with a huge bang. The TV followed it, only the power cable saved it from blowing into pieces. It was hanging a few centimetres above the debris.

"I don't think we can expect another quake in the next few hours," said the expert in the program, "because the seismometers would show prior signals."

Joshua wanted to laugh at this statement, but he couldn't; he felt a sharp pain around his diaphragm. He might have broken a rib. He wanted to sit up somehow, when another tremor pushed him back near the bed.

When he looked up, the kitchen wall was already in the middle of the room. It was dented like those containers in which somebody has created a vacuum. The furniture was bent, and plastic plates and cups were scattered across the floor.

Suddenly, it became dark: there was no sun and no light from the city.

The Big Trembling came, when everything went back to order. When the world of man vanished and God sent back the original rules. If somebody follows them he can start the race again.

He turned from his back onto his side, and pulled his leg up into a curled position. Plates and cups ran around him as the shock waves continued.

He gasped; his heart pumped faintly. The *Reanimator* would activate him again to bring him back from the short blackout.

But did it make sense? They might not find him under the ruins anymore. . . .

"Leave him!"
"Not until he asks for it loudly!"

He still heard the two separate voices in the continuous noise. They replied to each other: he could clearly identify both. As if they were the dark and white angels arguing over his soul. Both of them were his element. They lived in him always, but the black angel was more powerful, it had dominated throughout Joshua's life.

It was time to liberate the white angel. . . .

"Please . . ." He slowly pronounced the word he should have said long ago. His whisper was barely audible in the crash of trembling objects around him. But he felt an inner urge to do it. These might be his last sentences before his death if they didn't find him later. One day the food in the tubes would run out, the level of oxygen would drop—then the *Reanimator* would be helpless and useless.

"I beg you, don't judge me!" he said, gasping, struggling to say the words.

"Anybody against whom I've sinned, forgive me!"

Then the kitchen wall was drawn closer by another hit. Joshua slid to the leg of his bed in a contracted position.

"Humankind! My God!"

Then a small hole started to grow in the corner of the kitchen. A whistling noise came from it and became louder and louder. Suddenly, a big part was torn out of it and Joshua could see the night.

Joshua's shortness of breath became unbearable when the *Reanimator* kicked his heart for the last time.

"That's enough."

"Irene, my dear daughter, forgive me!"

The vacuum slowly sucked out all the air. Joshua's dead body was lifted up from the floor to the ceiling in weightlessness.

When the heating pipes had blown up, water flooded into the room. The floating bubble of water met with Joshua's body contracted into its foetal position. It surrounded him like a caul. When the room temperature descended to the coldness of space, the water became ice, preserving his body for eternity.

***

42 minutes earlier.

Francis Langen stood upright in front of the monitors. He had been a lawyer for nearly a hundred and seventy years, which meant that this was not his first successfully closed case.

"*Why did you reanimate him?*" he asked, outraged with the officer. The man in uniform pushed him to the holo-table with his chair. He asked for some data to be projected and pretended not to hear anything.

"Then I ask again: *why did you reanimate him?*" asked Francis, which made the guy angry, and he lifted his head up. He couldn't pretend anymore that Francis was not there. But he was still speechless and deep in the data tables.

"Look, if you still don't want to tell me *why you reanimated him*, then I'll sue you for abuse of professional power."

The guy finally turned to Francis after opening a document on the holo-table. There was no question that it was official: the circular stamp of the United Colony Tribunal of Justice fluoresced on it.

"So, look at this document, and please leave me alone. I need to prepare for the evacuation," said the officer sharply, and he turned back to the switches.

"*It was a huge mistake!* The lawsuit issued by my client has already overwritten this paper," said Francis, and he gave another holo-document to the guy.

The officer dawdled only a few seconds studying it, then threw it to the corner where it dissolved. "*One day or another doesn't mean anything* for an old man like him. The paper you've shown to me is only valid on Earth. That document I've shown you is issued by the United Colony Tribunal of Justice based on a lawsuit started by the claimant. . . ."

"What claimant? *However painful it is to admit it,* you decided it with your own competence. You are aware of the fact that all decisions made on the Mother Colony, on Earth, overwrite every decision on the colonies. It was always like that and will be in the future."

"But not here, in the periphery!"

Francis was flabbergasted by the statement. How could a man employed by the Solar System reject valid law? "I've been here for twenty-five damned years at Kuiper-belt, and I've had enough. And yes, I consider that countersigned document higher than any other you have. I don't care what he says, sue me! What can you gain by that? This shithole will be closed anyway and I will be out."

Francis started to realize that the officer's actions were motivated by his own anger and revenge. "I understand your feelings about losing your job," he said with a conciliatory tone in his voice, "but it isn't my client who is responsible for that. You have to understand: my client's actions in the past are not the implicit cause of the present situation on Earth and in the solar system."

The guy pointed at the screen instead of answering Francis. "I have no time to listen to your jumbled explanation. Do you see this patch here? This is the debris cloud remaining after the explosion of the Krayzfeld comet, which rejoined the Kuiper-belt seventy years ago. According to calculations, it will reach us soon. I would like to give you a small warning sign: the shields were deactivated two days ago. We only kept the complex in operation due to this client."

"I understand, it's as clear as the snow on that asteroid," nodded Francis. "But then explain to me: why did you reanimate him? *This is cruelty!*"

The eyes of the officer narrowed, as if he could kill with his glance. "I told you already: I did everything according to the papers!"

Francis saw no reason to continue arguing with him. He saw a better reason to leave this place as soon as he could, because the sensors—which were looking at the dangerous movement around the complex—filled the control room with bright red warning lights.

"My client has spent 82,325 days in the separation room. He has been confronted—by video programs—with his criminal actions on more than twelve thousand cases; crimes against humanity, crimes of getting financial gains by manipulating the span of human life, social and economic instability caused by an aging population... even though he has been discharged from all cases according to the document that you didn't take into account. According to the Tribunal statement, he and his product, the *Reanimator*, can't be the one and only cause of the catastrophic events that have happened on Earth. His capsule collided more than seven thousand times with other objects in the Kuiper-belt. The Central Computer explained these collisions with earthquakes about two thousand times..."

"Yes, exactly," said the officer, pushing a button to replay the newswoman's video feed, "and I will play back the same news spot about the earthquake again, because he'll soon be hit with the debris of the comet. Although I played this spot yesterday, this is our standard explanation."

"But why? Why are you doing this? My client's penalty was finished twenty-four years ago!" shouted Francis. "You can't simply ignore the law!"

The guy turned and went to the spacesuits. He opened the glass door and started to pull the suit on.

"If I were you, I would prepare; it's going to be tough. In one minute, we'll start getting the small pieces."

Francis looked at the docks where his ship rested. He had to fly the longest trip he'd ever taken to the Facility for Life-Sentenced of the United Colony Prison. The only prisoner there was his client, Professor Joshua Reehy, thus the authorities had decided to close the jail two months ago.

Francis was plagued by his conscience, as he had been since he got the message that his client hadn't been released. He could not ascertain the professor's freedom, as his legal matters kept him busy and away from this far end of the solar system.

Meanwhile, the first drifting debris hit Joshua's prison-capsule. The metallic container was no longer protected by the shields, so the collision dented its side, but it did not open yet.

Joshua's heart monitor showed abnormal values. The irregular beats followed each other more and more slowly as the tired muscles struggled to keep up after a few hundred years' work. The Central Computer gave another shot to the *Reanimator*.

"*Leave him!*" shouted Francis. "Stop it! You are not just breaking the law now, you're being cruel as well. Man, how can you do this? Doesn't it matter how he will end up? The asteroids will tear him to pieces. Let him go away!"

"*Not until he asks for it loudly!*" said the officer in a calm manner. Francis saw the deep emptiness in his eyes. He worked like a robot.

"What are you talking about? What does he need to say?"

The officer pointed to the database log of the computer. It contained all Joshua's pronounced words for all the years he had been kept there. A little piece of software, an algorithm that hunted for special words and expressions.

"What's this?" asked Francis, shocked. He felt that he should have received information about this action.

"This is the digital format of that document I showed to you earlier. Irene Reehy won a civil court case against her father—in which Joshua had been found guilty of the use of family members in dangerous experiments—and these words were included into the document's clauses."

Francis was speechless. This civil lawsuit was launched independently; he had no knowledge of it. He thought that the document was only one of the million lost civil cases that had been launched against the inventor of the *Reanimator*.

But it was not. He went closer to the holo-table to read the text. He was astonished.

Meanwhile, new pieces of icy balls collided with the unprotected floating prison. There was a huge dent on the corner of the container.

The Central Computer framed new words from the list.

"We are approaching!" said the officer and picked up his helmet. "Be prepared; we need to leave soon. The Central Computer stops all life-support systems in twelve minutes. Don't you use a spacesuit in your ship?"

Francis let the word fly past his ears. He didn't care about spacesuits; he stood there in his spotless, ironed, grey suit with matching tie. His client, Joshua, was the most famous prisoner, locked in for the longest time in human history. He had to show some respect.

The words "*humankind*" and "*my God*" were highlighted by the log program beside the expression "*forgive me*".
"Wouldn't have believed that he could say it . . ." The man shook his head after reading the words. He connected his helmet to the suit.
The heart monitor started to beep, indicating a serious heart condition for Joshua. Suddenly, a report plotted onto the screen, indicating that the program found eighty percent of the sought words; the computer waited for a human decision to continue. The officer hit the manual overdrive button without thinking and gave Joshua's *Reanimator* another shot.
"*That's enough!*" shouted Francis, already very angry. He touched his own *Reanimator*, it almost burned him from inside. The officer held up his hand to express that he was the master here. Francis stepped back.

Then a new expression appeared on the screen: "Irene, my dear daughter, forgive me!"

"That's it!" said the man shortly, then switched off the control panel.
At the same time the prison-container took a devastating hit from gigantic debris. There was a wide hole on its long side and something was flying through it into space. Francis hoped that Joshua couldn't see this anymore.
"Are you not coming? The base will have the same destiny in a few minutes." He pointed to the floundering remains of the prison-container. Francis grabbed his holo-tablet and headed after the guy.

"I am not so cruel," said the officer with an impish smile, "but I have a strange passion: I keep all rules even if they have no sense anymore."

"I see that clearly," said Francis, murmuring his words through his teeth. There was really no sense in keeping his client alive in this desperate situation, especially if the plaintiff—Joshua's daughter—had been dead for a century.

"In the end, everybody benefitted. The clause was fulfilled and your client is free now, isn't he?" said the guy in a spacesuit and tapped Francis on the shoulder.

Francis didn't say a word. He thought about Joshua's last moments and his freedom.

The officer stepped into an airlock and turned back for a last word before he closed the door:

"You can be proud of yourself. You were here when the most famous prisoner of humankind was freed. We don't let out a man *sentenced to lifelong life.*"

The airlock closed. The frozen vapor drew ice flowers on the circular window when the officer stepped into the cold of space.

Francis switched off the holo-table. Joshua's face—which was still floating in the air as a final picture—dissolved into eternity as the holo-picture slowly disappeared.

Life is the biggest burden, he thought, and fondled the bump on his chest. His *Reanimator* had been working for a hundred years without any problems. He was seventy when he bought it.

But he would not like to live for three hundred years.

That would be the real punishment.

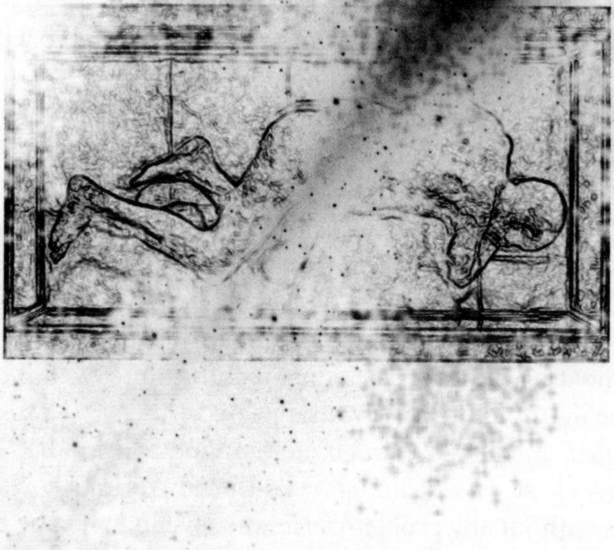

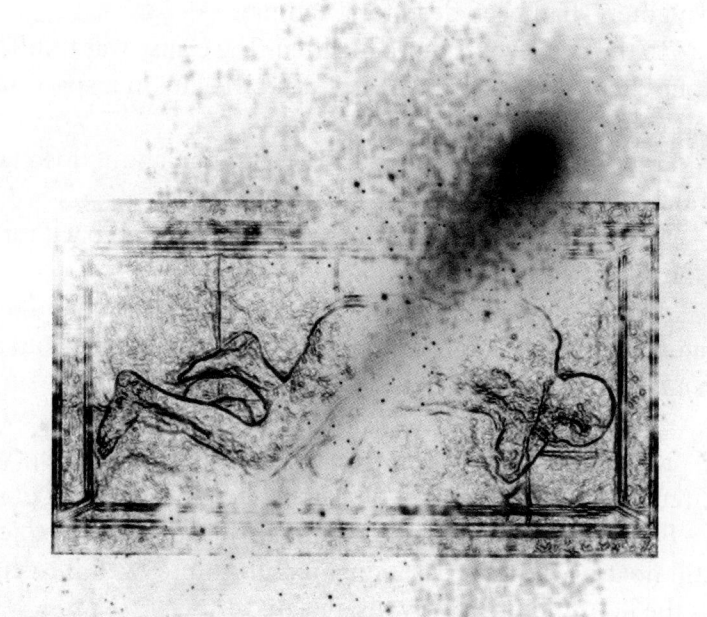

V.

Nothing but Comet Dust

The operation room of Infinite Space Independent Agency was a buzzing beehive, and it had reached its holding capacity; the whole world wanted to squeeze into that hall, seemingly spacious on any regular day.

Professor Greg Wiggerman, the flight director, looked up to the gallery where all the members of the colonial press fought for better places. There were only forty minutes left until the big events. The tension was tangible in the room, but also in his muscles—he was cramping from head to toe. Maybe if they moved on to the second phase, if they could just pass the approach successfully, if . . . he played out the scene in his mind. Even the cigarettes couldn't help; he'd smoked more than a pack in the past two hours.

"We'll change orbit twice in the next twenty minutes," the voice of his deputy, Jackson, pulled him back to reality. He sat at the neighboring desk and stared at the rows of numbers. "The data is coming in very well. There's no problem with the communication, batteries are all full, solar panels are opened, and we have enough fuel. I think we just have to wait for the right moment!" He smiled and knocked the glass cover of the clock above the control desk. The seconds trudged by slowly as if they carried lead weights. Jackson—seeing that his boss was more concerned than usual—squinted encouragingly at Greg.

"Take it easy!" he said, "this isn't our first mission. Think back to the seven successful ones we already did together."

Jackson was extremely and annoyingly optimistic. He had brazenly relaxed and easy manners, despite his age. Greg envied his nature. Even the boss could learn many things from his colleagues. A stress-relief technique would stand him in good stead right now.

"Yes, you're right. It's time for the real work already," said Wiggerman tensely and rubbed his face. He poured a cup of strong coffee from a thermos, pushed his chair to the monitors, and loosened his tie. At last, he took a deep breath and pushed the button of the intercom.

"Alright everybody, let's start with a little warm-up," he said and wiped the sweat from his balding head. "T minus 34 until the contact. I request maximum attention from all of you to do the work properly, as we've done several times before. We're a close-knit team. So, let's do it, c'mon!" His own applause filled the air after he finished his rousing speech.

"I need the report from each section," Jackson said, taking over. "Communication?"

"The antennas are turned toward the Earth, the line is clear and continuous."

"All right. Engines?"

"They are running well, fuel level corresponds to the prior estimated value," said a soft female voice from behind him. "It'll be enough for both the change on orbit and for landing too. For the return trip, we'll need a new calculation after the rendezvous, but if nothing goes wrong, it'll be enough. If there are any problems we'll reach Europa, as the orbit will be close to Jupiter."

"Perfect," said Greg, taking back the lead. "T minus 32 to contact. Sarah, you can start the press conference up there, please. You'll always be in my ear, I'll listen into your performance later." He tapped on the earplug in his left ear and waved up to the gallery. "Let's go, darling!"

"Thank you, boss, I'll change frequency but I'll watch you from above! So, good luck to everybody, and have a successful mission!" Static crepitated on the intercom when the press agent changed the line. A few second later, her voice came through the loudspeakers in the gallery, silencing the reporters. "Ladies and Gentlemen, we'd like to welcome you to the operational room of Infinite Space Independent Agency. We're very happy that you've joined us for this historical moment. Today we could have the answer to the universal question that has perhaps fumbled in all of our heads at least once in a lifetime, what humankind has always wanted to know: Where did the human race originate?"

The robot cameras flew around the room capturing flight controllers and engineers, and broadcasted their voices on every news channel across the Solar System.

"You can see all the details of the Genesis Project on the big screen, and on the left side we're showing you the live image—transmitted by the telescope, Giordano Bruno, orbiting around Jupiter. In the middle of this image we have the star of our show: the comet Glance-Blacksmith-Fenster. It's named after the three scientists who discovered it five months ago. It was only a blurred brush in front of the starry background. At first sight, the GBF was no more than a usual snowball, an icy rover visiting our Solar System. But it turned out to be a special one—a long-range traveller coming near to the sun only every two-and-a-half million years. This may have been the first ultra-long-range comet that humanity consciously observed in the sky."

She stayed silent for a few seconds to let the audience digest the information. Some might have come prepared; they could be bored for a moment. The most interesting part would come now. *A little repetition won't hurt, especially for outsiders,* thought Sarah.

Meanwhile, everything was going well in the operation room, the team had just passed the excitement of the first orbital correction. Greg, the flight director, looked ten years older as he stood behind the console.

Sarah continued the presentation:
"The Genesis Project is a multi-colonial effort; beside the Europa Colony, the Mother Colony—the Earth—and the Moon Colony are participating in the mission. As the comet GBF came closer to us, it revealed more and more of its true nature, but it still withheld its biggest secret—can a comet bear the components of life? Can the old theory be true: that comets spread life throughout the Solar System by colliding into the planets, taking the water and organic material to the surface?"

Yes, we're hunting for the big answer, thought Greg turning Sarah's voice down in the earplug. They were going for the "big fish", as they called the comet among themselves. That was why one of the idiots had put that stuffed fish on top of Greg's consol. He didn't object—it was a perfect motivation for a scientific fishing adventure.

When the scientists had found out that GBF was an ultra-long-range comet, the interest had greatly increased. The astronomical world had gone mad when they'd seen the first detailed analysis of the tail; it contained carbon and organic material alongside the icy dust. That was when they'd asked him, the well-known comet-hunter, to bring his team together. He had a remarkable portfolio; he'd made three successful space-rendezvous with hurtling celestial bodies.

This mission was more important than ever, so he'd enlarged his scientific team with big brains—involved some potentials from the United Colony Academy. His prestige was at stake, and he didn't want to take the responsibility on his own. Finally, the Genesis Board had asked him not only to organize, but to lead the Genesis Mission.

The icy rock had shown remarkable specialties right after its discovery; it continuously produced bright explosions of light. Telescope Giordano Bruno had discovered it in the process of looking for supernovae blasts by photographing the specified slides of the far universe. The scientists had thought it couldn't be a supernova—it was definitely changing its position, so it could not be a trace of a dying star. The GBF had left no doubt; it was the strangest comet ever seen heading towards the Solar System.

The GBF did not stop producing the spectacular lightshow; it was a real headache to the scientists who wanted to unravel the phenomenon. These kinds of flashes normally happened when the gas—trapped inside the rock—burst to the surface, induced by the solar wind. But when those blasts started, the GBF was very far from the sun, where the effect of the solar wind was negligible. This behavior generated endless disputes within the scientific circles, but the snowball did not care about it; it continued to be unusual.

A few months later, the solar wind stuck an amazing tail to the wanderer. It was an extraordinary sight that everyone wanted to see. The best view of the bright blue-white tail was from Jupiter's moon, Europa; the travel agencies sold a lot of tickets to the observation stations orbiting around Jupiter. Then suddenly, the flashes stopped, although the scientists had expected just the opposite—the mysterious visitor didn't want to be ordinary. It was unique in another way too: it came with a very wide angle to the plane of the Solar System.

When everybody accepted its unconventional behavior, it twisted the expectations around again; it changed its course. It did not exhibit the usual "good boy" attitude of a house-sized comet—the course change might have been accounted for if it had grazed next to a planet with strong gravitational forces or collided with debris, but neither happened. It traveled through the abandoned area of the Solar System.

That was the time when they started to whisper about a non man-made object. The comet was rumored to be a camouflage, hiding an alien spaceship behind its mask. It was never hard to find a sci-fi maniac or reporter hungry for sensations who fed this belief. But the tempers cooled suddenly when the telescope Giordano Bruno proved it, that the comet Glance-Blacksmith-Fenster was no different from any other comets that had drawn beautiful tails in the night sky centuries before. It was only a barren, ice-hearted wanderer, but everybody admitted—it was one of the special ones.

A few weeks later, the sensation hit the news: the scientists had finished their analysis of the composition of the tail—it contained the spectrum of amino acids' hydrogen bond, compound of amino acids, phosphorus beside the compound carbon and water.

This discovery brought the old panspermia theory to light again. People looked into old books, reading about the comets flying like giant spermium to impregnate the protoplanets with the seed of life.

The news was full of dilettantes who came out with ridiculous plans to catch the comet. In response, Greg hired two new specialists to his team; both of them were experts in the field of Xenobiology. Greg commissioned them to make a scientific plan for collecting data and samples from the comet, based on their experiences in the studies of the exoplanets.

In the past five months, they had launched four satellites in the direction of GBF. Three of them flew from Europa, one from the Moon—saving the high cost of the orbital launch from the Earth. Launching from Europa saved time too—they got within arm's length of the GBF.

Twenty-four minutes to reach it with our fingertips, thought Greg as he looked up at the mission clock. Only a tight half-hour left until the Hugo landing phase at the rendezvous point.

"Take it easy, boss, Hugo is watching over you at the moment. He has a wide line of sight on the events, including you, from above somewhere," said Jackson, spreading his arms wide, hovering above the consoles and imitating total control. It was frightening how well he could read Greg's mind. Greg thought about his dad, Hugo Wiggerman, who was the biggest name in the astronomical world in the past fifty years. He changed space exploration with his revolutionary inventions, giving a new type of rocket engine and energy cells to humankind. Greg had named the comet-lander after his father. When the probe reached the comet, it would complete his father's last wish—his ashes, in a thimble-sized jar, would be placed on the surface of the wanderer.

There was intense argument about this decision behind the scenes—many scientists were against it. Their concerns were logical; they wanted to find the trace of the life on this icy rock.

"We can't contaminate it by placing human remains on the target of our own scientific experiment," said many of them. Finally Greg had convinced them that the sealed jar would not endanger the success of the experiment—it would not open or become damaged during the landing.

"T minus 18 to the rendezvous point," said Jackson. Greg returned to his seat and tried to clear his mind of the old memories and concentrate only on the task.

"Minus 4 to the next change of orbit," Greg took over. "Engines?"

"They're all fine, fuel level as expected, we're ready!" answered the engineer responsible for the propulsion system.

"All right then, T minus 3 and we can start. I need full concentration. There is no second chance. If we miss, then the Hugo falls behind the comet and we can say goodbye to the rendezvous. We will have only two minutes for correction, otherwise the signal won't reach the probe in time. So I'll start the countdown: one-fifty-nine, one-fifty-eight, one-fifty-seven . . .

*

Siol Rebina was very nervous. As the Monarch's first secretary, she had never been given such a big responsibility before. This was the deepest mourning there had ever been in the realm. The fulfilment of the task imposed an almost unbearable burden on her. The anxiety and pressure was so intense that it induced physical pain in her mind.

She'd been working continuously for four weeks. She'd gathered around her an infallible cast of trustworthy scientists. She needed their expertise in the perfect preparation. The Monarch was not in the right state of mind to survive an accidental fiasco. His rage would break through every floodgate. Siol had seen his anger and pain in the past ten-and-a-half months. That was the ten-and-a-half months' tribulation. And there was no mercy for sinners in the time of tribulation.

It was two weeks ago when they had left the Nebra and gone through the hypergate. The door just opened to the other side of space like it had several times before; they hadn't made any mistakes in the calculations. They were exactly where they wanted to be—in the middle of the comet's tail.

Remote observers could see only several bright bursts of light; once, when space turned into itself and opened a wormhole to the other universe, and for a second time when space flattened again. They could perceive no more; the Monarch's cruiser was hidden inside the white-hot coma. There was also a cloaking shield, which made sure that the ship stayed invisible for any detection device. They were flying toward the only habitable planet, so the comet's core beneficially concealed them too.

The Monarch himself had chosen this comet. This was an average, non-ostentatious, long-range wanderer that was completely fit for the purpose. Its course passed through remote, deep space where there was no problem opening the hypergate. So, when the mission was over and they circled the Sun, they would be invisible and could open the wormhole again and let the comet into their universe. The beautiful visitor could start its few months of splendor, making an appearance even more than once a year—or in the rhythm of the Monarch's favor. Then, finally, the Monarch could find his peace, and rest in the memories.

Later on, they could let the comet back to this side of space.

They wanted to open the gate close to the Mother System. The Monarch held deep respect for the spirit of his ancestors, so he thought that the Mother System was the most suitable place for the funeral rites. The blue planet—with its oceans and massive, continuous continent—was in hundreds of Nebra's legends, and heroic songs chanted its ancient wonders, when it was inhabited by an intelligent species. The stories mentioned that it was forbidden to return to the Mother System after the last wave of emigration. The place, from which all Nebras originated, had to stay intact, therefore this was the first time they had opened the hypergate since the big migration. They only broke this prohibition for spiritual reasons. Siol, the first secretary, got a mandate to do this—she was so excited to come to her ancestor's system.

They could keep their arrival a secret because the satellite, which drove the hypergate, could open a ship-sized hole in the vicinity of the huge gas planets. It used and transformed the gravitational force of these mighty planets as a never-ending energy source; it was working without maintenance for millions of years.

They had just passed the big Rihane-seru—the Double-Red-Eyes, as they called the gas giant, the fifth planet, orbiting in the Mother System. Although, Siol noticed, only one huge red spot turning around the equator was visible—the other super storm could have dissolved in the atmosphere already.

After leaving the hypergate, Siol had received a sobering warning: the Blue Planet had become inhabited again. Siol launched a cloaked probe, which confirmed there was another birth from the womb of the Mother Planet, and a new intelligent species had been created by Almighty God. According to the sensors, the species had achieved space travel—it left the blue planet and flew through the Solar System. Siol found traces of intelligent life—meaningful data—that originated from the moon of the gas giant and the red planet. They had received not only automatic, scientific data from probes but bits following musical patterns too. From this discovery, Siol realized that the new species had created colonies in the Mother System.

This fact made her worried. She couldn't change the plan, because it might put the Monarch into a deeper crisis if the new species discovered them. But she had taken a precautionary measure; she'd changed the comet's course—pushing it further from the inhabited moon of the gas giant—by blasting two energy charges. With God's protection—and with the deployment of their entire technical arsenal—they could stay unseen until the rite was finished.

They had prepared for the funeral rite for one-and-a-half months. The child, a long-awaited crown prince, whose birth had been foretold years ago (*"his name will be Pios-Raya, Golden Bridge"*), who would make connections from the Nebra to the blue planet of the ancestors; *he was stillborn.* He took his mother, Nebra's wonderful dawn, with him into the other world...

The Monarch descended into a deep melancholy, then suddenly rose to the heavens of momentum where he threw himself into organizing the ceremony. With the help of his scientist, he found the comet that was used to travel through the hypergate between the two universes, and planned to throw their remains into two Solar Systems.

Siol had to prepare everything on the comet approaching the Mother System; that's why she was there in the coma. The Monarch and the royal family would arrive later with six bigger ships. The royal ships would hide in the coma following the comet—as the funeral procession. Then they would let the icy rock turn around the sun and open the gate into deep space, to let the Pios-Raya—the comet would be named after the crown prince—appear in the night sky of the Nebra.

She was ready to receive the royal family. They would open the gate in thirty minutes, as they were still far enough from the Blue Planet to be able to finish the rite on time.

A rain of dust and millions of ice fragments hit the outside camera, which sent the images to the main screen. Siol involuntarily squinted, watching the micro-sized particles racing toward her. *The stardust of the predecessors*, she thought, when the first officer stepped beside her.

"Lady Siol," he sounded concerned, "we've just localized a probe approaching from the other side of the comet. It's on a collision course. The creators may want to land on or—more possibly—collide with the comet. It must be an experimental mission, we've done something similar before."

"Almighty God . . ." moaned the woman. Her posture swayed a bit. She was dead tired, she'd thought she was over all the hardship—she'd counted on everything except this. It would be disastrous if the new inhabitants of the blue planet hit the comet in the middle of the funeral.

An orange-red wave rushed through her brown skin from her face to her neck, a sign of stress, and she rubbed the squamas of her hands together nervously. The officer stood patiently next to her.

"We can't stop now. I want two armed, cloaked droids stationed on both sides of the comet. In case of any threat, blow it up."

The officer ran back to his post on the bridge and took immediate action, instructing the computer to calculate the course of the droids.

At exactly the same moment, the buzz sounded to warn them about opening the hypergate. Siol shuddered.

*

Greg Wiggerman froze into a statue when he saw the first images coming with a two-minute delay from the Hugo. The Glance-Blacksmith-Fenster was the most beautiful comet he'd ever seen. It was not only beautiful but special too; it looked like there was something else—might be another core, a rock—in the coma. The dust and debris coming from the surface hid everything from plain sight, but the radars saw; something was there to divert the particles.

The tail was unusually wide and short from Earth's viewpoint—as the solar wind blew the tail to the opposite direction. But on the Hugo's cameras and on the Giordano's pictures, it looked magnificent.

The final worthy place for my father's remains, thought Greg. He'd wanted this. Wanted to be part of the Universe, when his atoms would be joined again into the big circulation . . .

He's up there, happy, and watching us.

"T minus 11 until the rendezvous," said Jackson, on his right. "According to telemetry, the course is perfect. There is enough fuel to land, take samples, and say goodbye to Professor Hugo Wiggerman," he added, looking meaningfully at Greg. Jackson loved Greg's father, the professor's death had left deep scars on him too. "Then the orbital phase will fly through the tail, gathering samples. If it runs out of fuel, we'll catch it around the orbit of Jupiter."

Meanwhile in the gallery, Sarah continued to inform the press. Her voice could be heard faintly through the glass.

"The task is huge; the scientists had to calculate the course of the Hugo very precisely. Even half a meter calculation difference can cause a ten, twenty, or hundred kilometre difference after travelling thousands of kilometres. The next few minutes will be the cornerstone of the mission: Will the rendezvous be established? Can we obtain samples from the tail? Will the preliminary result of the spectral analysis—meaning are there organic components on it—be justified?"

When she finished the sentence, the big screen filled with white flashes. The pictures disappeared; all data went crazy and then stopped. The Hugo was silenced.

"What happened?" asked Greg. "Did we lose it? Telemetry, what's going on with the data?"

"I have no idea," answered the engineer. "The Hugo is blind and deaf. It's possible we lost it."

"Let's not jump to conclusions too soon. The data flow can be recovered. We have the radar data from the Europa, where we can still see the probe," said somebody hopefully.

"But it was more than two minutes ago," Greg shook his head. "Switch immediately to the picture from Giordano."

The big screen got dark for several seconds then slowly came back to life. There was an incredibly amazing scene playing out. Many people jumped from their seats and ran through the hall.

"It looks like the comet broke into several pieces," said Jackson, composed, the first among them to wake up from their dismay. "According to radar data, there are six separate pieces that exploded out from the core. The accumulated gas could have caused it."

The audience at the gallery bombarded Sarah with questions once they recovered from their astonishment, and the engineers stuck to their monitors to see the particles bouncing away from the smaller pieces.

"All data recovered from Hugo, the probe is live again!" said an engineer, followed by exploding cheers from all over the room.

"Then back to places! We continue the approach. Telemetry, was there any change in course?"

"Negative. Both courses are stable: neither the comet nor the Hugo deviated."

"All right, go for it! T minus 7 to the rendezvous. Let's get the big fish!"

Greg's voice was replaced by the click of the keyboard as everyone turned back to their task. Only Sarah's commentary went on the public channel:

"What you've just seen a few minutes ago has already been experienced in the history of comet research. The most famous event was in 1993, when the comet Shoemaker-Levy 9 exploded because of the gravitational force of Jupiter. It fell into the gas giant, and the predecessor of the Giordano Space Telescope, the Hubble, recorded it. You can see on the left side . . ."

*

The royal ships dropped out of hyperspace with several bright blasts. The gate was only open for thirty seconds, but it was enough time for all the ships to come through. The fleet gathered in the coma formed random patterns as if they had blasted down from the original core. This was the most critical part of the whole plan. All ships switched on their cloaking device, only the continuously showering dust and ice outlined their uncertain forms. It was impossible to detect their real presence.

Siol made sure that the intercom's broadcast would not go to the outside space and opened the channel.

The figure of Kilehu, the Monarch, filled the cruiser's main screen on the bridge. He radiated orderliness and tranquillity. His lateral gill plate—a peculiarity of amphibians—was lifting and descending in a stress-free rhythm. He looked totally prepared for the event, like he had gained back his mental balance.

"I salute you, my dear secretary, Siol. I thank you for your sacrificial work, as you've spared no effort to organize everything. You are a true blessing to me."

Siol didn't know what to say. Instead she bent her knee politely, as the custom dictated. Her gill plates pumped the air quickly, she could not dissemble her anxiety.

"Your Highness, be welcomed in the System of our ancestors, in the Mother System. It was my honor that you chose me, I am humbled. If you are ready, we can start the ceremony."

The Monarch bowed his head, gaining strength for a second and then nodded.

"Let us begin . . ." he said.

On Siol's signal, the lead royal ship went well inside the coma, right beside the core. During the graceful manoeuvre, the sounds of fanfare filled all the cruisers. There was a wide, grieving crowd on board, surrounding the two capsules that stood on a pulpit. Friends and relatives joined them from the other cruiser virtually, in holographic form.

The Monarch walked into the gap between the capsules, pulling his hand over the engraved ornaments on the surface. These engravings were from the legends of Nebra; they represented the tree of life embracing the lifelike portraits of his son and wife. The capsules were made from quickly decomposing material, which would let the ashes spread on the turbulent surface of the comet.

They would take the tears of the Monarch too. Kilehu stooped over the remains of his family, letting his tears fall down—teardrops ran deep down into the grooves and outlined the form of pain. Two huge branches had broken from the tree of life a few months ago.

He straightened up slowly, knelt down, and raised his hands; he started to pray. Siol signaled to the crew. The capsules started to move toward the torpedo tubes—the Monarch's salty teardrops helped them to slide along the rails. The blackness of the tubes swallowed them and, after a low hissing sound, they departed for the surface.

Siol had programed the torpedo tubes so that the capsules could circle around each other in a continuously descending spiral. They would meet and become one with each other and with the dust of the comet. They would be together for all eternity, as the Monarch had requested.

As planned, the two capsules danced with each other in a marvellous way. The comet dust wove a silken veil around them, circled like two brides in the revival dance of death. At the end, the mother embraced her child again, holding him for a moment, when they finally became one.

In the next moment, the capsules disintegrated and reached the surface. The ashes were united with the dust of the comet and the ancestors.

It's all finished, thought Siol, sighing. Her heart still pumped like a machine, but she was extremely happy that all went well.

The mourners watched the pelting particles in a cold, perishing silence. Only Kilehu's faint cry could be heard from the background.

*

"Only twelve seconds," said Jackson. "The sampling unit is ready. Greg?"
"Yes, I'm ready too. Thank you." Greg knew that he had to compose himself; the whole world was watching him.
"I want to thank everybody who made this final tribute possible," he said, clearing his throat. "Hugo Wiggerman, father, brilliant scientist; your earthly passage has come to an end. You have been a bright star in the sky of the scientific world. You can be the new wanderer in the universe."
He took off his glasses and wiped a tear from the corner of his eyes.
"Rest in peace!" he said, pushing the button to launch the capsule that contained his father's ashes. When he looked up, all the people were on their feet bowing their heads before his father's memory.
"The capsule reached the surface beside the sampling unit, which is already on the way back," commented Jackson.

"Thank you, all of you," said Greg. "Let's launch the overflying unit through the tail, and hope it won't hit anything there."

*

Siol was preparing to finish the ceremony when the alarm went off.

"The alien probe launched a small unit accelerated by a rocket engine. They probably want to go to the tail. We need to annihilate it, otherwise they will discover us or damage the ships."

"No," answered Siol. "Notify the cruisers, we go to hyperspace. The gates should be open in twelve seconds."

"I understand. Wormhole opens in twelve seconds."

Oh, God, just in time, thought Siol.

*

Greg and the team saw the bright, flashing phenomenon. The previously torn pieces of the core could blow up, because they hadn't seen them on the Giordano's pictures. It could also be that Jupiter's mighty gravitational force deviated and disintegrated these icy rocks.

They'd lost the sampling unit driven through the tail, and they couldn't find the Hugo either. Only the landing sampler survived and it was on its way back to Jupiter. The secret of the comet would soon be revealed.

"Have a good journey, Dad. I will always love you," said Greg, looking after the comet.

The hall filled with applause despite the losses.

*

Siol sat at the Salon. She had really good news for the Monarch. Pios-Raya, the Golden Bridge, fulfilled the prophecy; he made contact with the new species of the Mother planet. They called themselves *humankind*, according to the decoded and broadcasted transmissions.

And this was not the only good news. According to the research they had made in deep space, the humans had used this comet for a funeral too. Their scientists had found a small capsule on the surface that contained carbon-based organic remains.

They were common. The ancestors, humans, and Nebranians.

. . .

God works in mysterious ways, but his prophecies will be fulfilled, she thought right at the moment when the valet came to lead her into the room of the Monarch.

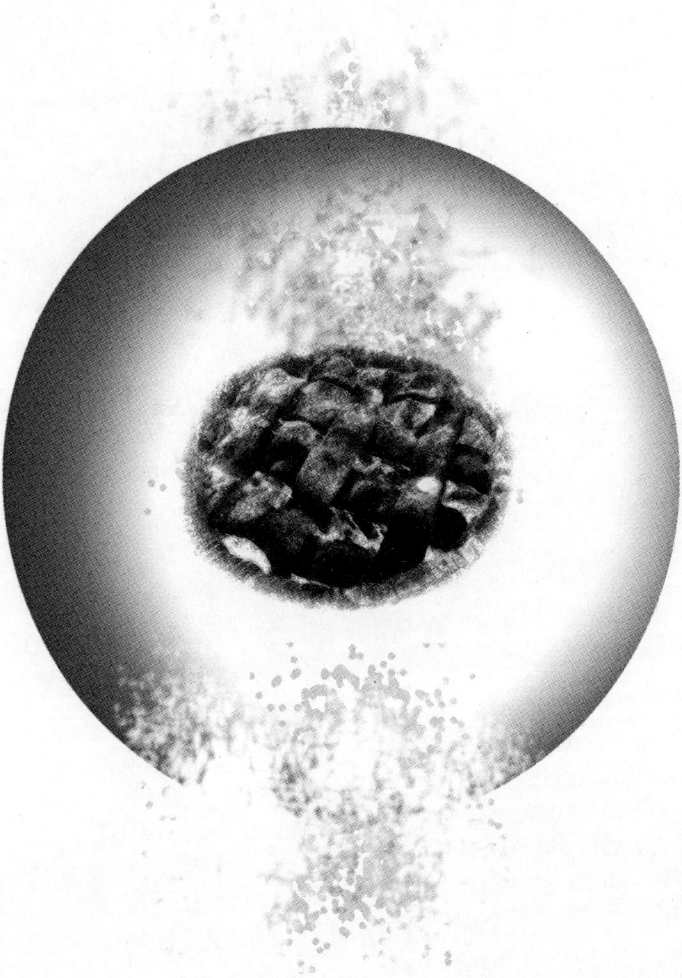

VI.

Parallel Juridical Process

"No, I don't claim to have seen Jack in church much, but that doesn't rule out that he believed in God," said Reverend Delgado, sipping his coffee. His answer was directed at Mrs. Malcolm, who had a doubt about the deceased's salvation. "The issue of salvation is a very complex question," he added, and tried to distance himself from the conversation, to find somebody else who was not so insistent, who wouldn't cling to him like a leech. The funeral feast had already been going on for thirty minutes, but he could not stop this lady's unpleasantness.

"I went fishing with him a lot. He mentioned God's name all the time, although not nicely," laughed Bill, the neighbour. "Excuse me, Reverend, but you know, the late Jack liked to swear if the fish got away from him, when it snapped the line. But who can hold himself back after a disaster like that?" grinned Bill and took liberties tapping the reverend's shoulder.

Bill may be cracking his usual tasteless joke, Reverend Delgado thought, *but at least I'm saved from Mrs. Malcolm's endless discussion, it could go on through the next four funerals.*

"I understand, Bill, I know it happens a lot, but we should not take God's name in vain," said the reverend, turning to Bill. Mrs. Malcolm was deeply disappointed as she retreated into the crowd. Bill was not a brilliant partner for a witty chat either, but he wouldn't bring up the same topic over and over again at every funeral as Mrs. Malcolm did. If we cannot prove something, we don't need to waste so much time on it; this was the reverend's opinion. It is better that we stand still in our faith.

"Believe me, I am just acting like a stupid clown, but I was indisposed by his death," added the neighbour. "It wasn't his time yet..."

They hemmed and hawed, stamped around; nobody could say a word for a short time, everybody was embarrassed.

"Now, in the twenty-third century, people don't get excited about faith, do they, Reverend?" A young, well-dressed man stepped into the circle. He took a piece of the strawberry jelly cake that was attracting the most guests. There wasn't much left on the tray.

"Excuse me, let me introduce myself. I'm David Fincher."

"Nice to meet you, Mr. Fincher," nodded the reverend. "But I don't think we need to throw away our faith for something tactile and sacrifice on the altar of gadgets. The existence of these technical devices only proves that God gave us free will to discover the boundaries of our talent. Look, I also use one of these," he took a small cylindrical object from his cassock. "This is a memo-device. It doesn't make sound or show any pictures, but uses nonconventional methods to communicate..." he fell silent, embarrassed, "and I have to admit I have no idea how it works. I use it because I need it for my old, skipping brain, but I have a strange feeling about it. It's something alien to me."

"This technique was called telepathy in the past, nowadays we call it *wave-communication*, although a lot of people dislike that expression," said a young woman stepping into the circle. She had waist-length, blonde hair with a wide black ribbon twisted around it. "We use these gadgets to cheat on the exams at school, although they covered all the auditoriums to shield against it. I got it from Uncle Jack . . ." her voice faltered when she pronounced the name of her late relative "so he bought me that one a while ago."

Everyone just stood there, staring uncomfortably at their shoes while the circle got bigger and bigger. The strawberry jelly cake used a wave-communication-like effect by disseminating its mouth-watering aroma into the room. More and more people came around and fought for the last pieces.

"The good old jelly cake does the job, doesn't it? It calls the people together better than any gadget," said Tim Carlson, the grocer from the neighbouring street. His grandfather had opened a little, traditional family shop that Tim changed to a popular delivery discount. The customers could order from their armchairs, and robotic floating carts delivered the fresh goods to their door.

"You still changed the shop," said Bill with the usual giggle, "even though my Granny loved the Saturday afternoons when your Granddad put out that sign 'Jump in for a chat'. They sat there talking for hours and redeeming the world. That was a more humane society!"

"All right, I admit it," answered Tim, taking a big bite of the special cake, "but who wants to spend time chatting in a grocery store nowadays? All the youngsters sit in virtual cafes. I can't keep a shop only for chatting!"

"My dears!" a trilling voice came suddenly into the circle. The owner of the voice was a woman in a tight black, mid-length skirt, and was followed by Reverend Delgado's reproachful look. Many became confused; they could not decide between watching the shapely legs emerging from below the mini-skirt or taking another jelly cake from the full tray held by the woman. She, Mary Spencer, the *Merry Widow* as they called her, was the wife of the deceased, although they had been separated for years. The divorce was pending because Jack didn't want it. Mary became the heir now; she could expect half of the floating-car salon's shares. The other half were claimed by Sao, Jack's alleged son and Mary's stepson, who had popped up from nowhere. *The Merry Widow* had attempted to get his shares too. There were delusive values below her attractive looks.

"Mary, you are gorgeous even in this deep mourning," said the man who had introduced himself as David Fincher, shaking her hand. "I'm a friend of your son, he invited me. Don't you see him?"

"Do you mean Sao?" asked Mary, disturbed, while she slid the second tray over the empty one. "No, he's not my son. He's my alleged stepson, but only alleged! He issued a lawsuit for my husband's properties a few months ago, saying that he's Jack's unknown son. I have serious doubts about it," she added with a resentful expression. "Try to find him in the kitchen. I saw him somewhere over there."

"You are so kind. I would rather wait here," said Mr. Fincher politely. "I don't want to wander around in somebody else's house just like that."

"As you wish . . . Oh, Bill, so you came finally!" she turned to the neighbour. "Thank you for coming. I know you haven't had a good relationship with Jack in the past years. It's so generous that you honoured him—I mean his memory."

It wasn't a good relationship? thought Tim, the grocer, of course it wasn't. *It was an open secret that you had a relationship with Bill first. Then I was your next prey, until you threw me out. Who is it now? Is it that guy in the black suit—he had a bag in his hand, he must be a travelling agent—stood back of the room? You always loved the affairs. I'm sure you have somebody to keep you in good shape. Otherwise you wouldn't look so seductive . . .*

"My dears, unfortunately I have to leave you to pick up some refreshments from the kitchen. Continue your conversation and enjoy my homemade jelly cake," said a quavering Mrs. Spencer and left them alone. Men were looking mesmerized after the spectacular receding legs for a few seconds then they all pounced on the cake. The circle narrowed and dilated, pulsated rhythmically like a living jellyfish. The strawberry jelly cake did its best—made all the guests quiet for a short time. The ghost of Jack Spencer would feel quite at home if he were there.

Then Mary's sudden scream broke that intimate silence. It was right before two sequential events, first a loud thud (*Mary must have fainted*, thought Bill, who had witnessed Mary going haywire before), then a sharp clink (*and the plates landing on the floor next to her*).

The crowd circled her while small screams and excited shouts filled the air. Some people pointed to the kitchen, others whispered with shocked voices: "It's impossible, we've just buried him!"

There was a blue, pervasive light coming out of the kitchen. It had some kind of definite contour, just like the jelly fondant. What's more, it looked exactly like the jelly on the top of the cake. In the middle of it, a man—who looked like the late Jack from behind—was sitting beside the kitchen table. A faint tingling murmur—like a cold chill—ran through the people standing around.

The well-dressed man with the suitcase was sitting in the corner of the kitchen now. There was a little table in front of him covered by blinking buttons and slider switches—it looked like some kind of keyboard. It also had a small, foldable screen attached to its side.

An Asian man was standing beside him; he was Sao, Jack's alleged son. He couldn't participate in the rite due to the remonstrance of the widow and the relatives, but he was allowed to enter the house, at least. Sao brought a court order, stating he had a right to stay in the house during the period of the investigation, and nobody wanted to argue with an official document.

"Dear ladies and gentlemen, let me introduce myself: I am David Fincher, working for the County Prosecutor's Office as a forensic detective dealing with financial crimes. I was asked to carry out a juridical demonstration process in this inheritance case. As the lawsuit enters the investigative phase, we have to prove or confute the statement of Mr. Sao Vaotang—claiming he is the legitimate son of the deceased, Mr. Jack Spencer. That is why we are here with you today."

He left a short pause for the *mourners* to recover from the primary shock, although this was not enough for Tim. He thought he could only wake up from this strange dream by a horse kick or a strong drink.

"We deeply apologize for the turmoil and inconvenience, but we are in a hurry; we don't have much time to accomplish our goals. First of all, because Madame Spencer is presumably prepared to leave soon—she bought a ticket to the ferry departing to the Moon this evening. We were informed that she sold the floating-car saloon—although it was impounded by the court before—yesterday afternoon and wanted to leave the Earth with this money. Am I right, Mrs. Spencer?" Mr. Fincher asked the widow, who was helped into a chair in front of the kitchen door. She was quite dizzy, so the question was still hanging in the air. The forensic detective continued, "Secondly, we are in a hurry due to the nature of this very new invention we are trying to use for the first time."

He stepped next to the man sitting in front of the switchboard.

"My colleague, Mr. Weakman, will help me run this investigation. What you can see here is a Parallel Space-bending Device. Up until now, it's only been used for experimental purposes, but the time has come to harvest the fruits of that long development process."

The living room was absolutely silent. Only a sharp clank—caused by a fallen fork—sounded through it, but nobody turned a head in that direction. Bill, the neighbour, struggled and croaked, swallowing the last piece of the cake in his mouth, which was already dry due to the unexpected events.

"The substance before you is the closed drop of an existing parallel reality. This drop has been torn from a parallel universe—from the existing present there—and placed into our reality. The man in the other world, namely Jack Spencer"—the crowd roared when the name was mentioned—"does not follow the destiny he had here. Obviously, he is alive and having dinner in the same type of kitchen we have here. This is very good news for us, who are working for justice. We were not sure that we'd find him alive in one of the parallel realities, so that's why we had to act so quickly."

He pointed theatrically to the huge, blue jelly bulb.

"But, as you can see, after looking through twenty-five existing realities, we've finally found not only an empty kitchen, but a living man! I don't want to waste time describing our findings in the other twenty-four universes, but there were some in which this kitchen didn't even exist. In those universes, the past had diverted long ago. If Jack exists in those universes, he could be somewhere else, in another city, but not here. So, based on this logic, I think we're on the right track now, I don't know if you're still following me . . ."

It was unclear whether the guests were following him or not. They were still in the same stiff positions from the beginning of the event and were looking at the pulsating bubble in disbelief. The afternoon had taken on the feeling of a hypnotic séance for them.

"Then I'll continue describing the lawsuit submitted by Mr. Sao Vaotang—from now on named Mr. Spencer, as he recently took up his alleged father's name. Mr. Spencer stated that he was born with the aid of artificial conception from the late Jack Spencer's sperm. Due to this legal reason, he claims the equal share of the following assets: Moonlight Floating Car Rental, The Best Models floating-car saloon, and twelve percent ownership in shares of Outer Rim Power Plants. He would hold fifty percent ownership of all aforementioned properties in case of successful demonstration today."

Mary Spencer had gotten a coffee in the meantime, and two relatives were trying to hold her in the chair. She was speechlessly watching her husband sitting—and eating some kind of meat with vegetables—in the middle of the blue blob. Her mesmerized eyes looked pallid, gazing into the middle of the surrealistic event.

"Before somebody raises a completely valid question about why we didn't make a simple test to prove the genetic relationship between Mr. Jack and Sao Spencer, my answer is that this is not possible anymore, as Mr. Spencer's body has been atomized. This happened on the request of Madame Spencer, who told the officials that atomization was the last wish of Mr. Spencer. Thus, Mr. Sao Spencer had no chance to say a final farewell to his father, who died in the hospital of an unknown disease. We could not find the cause of the deadly illness, as it had rapidly killed the victim."

The audience started to fidget as Jack, in the glowing, blue parallel world, stood up in the kitchen. He took more—obviously Asian—food from a takeaway paper box with his chopsticks, and then went back to his chair.

At this moment the technician, Mr. Weakman, turned something on the console in front of him, because the bubble became clearer: Jack's face could be seen perfectly. The mourners watched him with wide eyes—Jack's skin was covered with scabs like semi-healed pockmarks. He looked awful, so a few faint-hearted turned their backs to him, heading to the far end of the living room.

But nobody had left the house so far; everybody wanted to see the outcome of this strange funeral reception.

"If any of you are worried that he can see or hear us, I can assure you that it cannot happen. Although Mr. Weakman is able to change the settings so that we could interfere in the other world—for instance, we could move things on the table without being seen, as if we were a poltergeist—we will not demonstrate those abilities here."

Meanwhile, Jack finished his dinner and poured the leftovers into a machine (Bill, the neighbour thought it was some kind of food waste dispenser, which was less advanced than the same equipment in this world), then he suddenly left the bubble—and the scope—in the direction of the living room. Mr. Weakman briskly jumped from his small chair (which was connected to the console), rolling his equipment into the corner of the living room. The black-clad spectators fled from him, giving away their fear.

"I would like to ask everybody to move closer to the walls, in order to have more space for the parallel bubble to move and continue the investigation."

The technician's fingers were quick. After pushing some keys, he slowly turned one of the switches. The bubble, like a giant jellybean, wandered through the doorway then finally stopped in the middle of the living room. It didn't leave much space for the mourners (although, to name them mourners was already pointless, as Jack was fiddling with the remote control in front of them—alive and kicking, as if he hadn't been the subject of a funeral ceremony just a few hours before).

Some were frightened when the blue substance touched their shoes, but Mr. Fincher assured everyone that no fatal event would happen to them. The widow (this term was also bizarre under the circumstances) was close to the copy of her husband, sitting at the edge of the couch, already halfway into the blue bubble—she didn't care about that. She pulled herself together for the moment, waiting there with a provocative expression on her face, anxious to see what would happen.

Sao Spencer was still standing beside the technician with an emotionless, unblinking face.

Jack sunk down into an armchair (this piece of furniture was not at the same place as the furniture in this world, and it was an old-fashioned, worn type—with several holes in the armrest). There was a *gameshow* on the TV (in the old, tube version TV with pallid colours), and Jack was shouting continually at the participant, although nobody could hear his voice in this present. He slapped his knee and beat the table with the remote whenever the player failed to give the correct answer. Sometimes he took a handkerchief, dipped it into some kind of liquid, and then cleaned the scabs on his face.

Suddenly, he switched off the TV and rushed to the front door.

"We can only hope that he will not leave the house, because we're not able to follow him there. Unfortunately, this invention only has limited possibilities. Mr. Weakman, if you would be so kind . . ." said Fincher, pointing to the hallway. Mr. Weakman was so kind to set his switches to the right direction, and the bubble had followed Jack Spencer. It was right on time, because he opened the door. The black-dressed *army of mourners* fled away from him—it was unnecessary, as they lived in a totally different universe.

There were some people who left the house at the same moment, mostly those who were with their small children or simply got fed up with the excitement. They opened the door in this reality, and stepped out into the street of this world.

Jack stood at the doorway for a moment then made way for a young man and a middle-aged woman. All three came into the living room and stood there—the guests of this world groaned as the young man looked like a younger version of Sao. The slight difference of the two versions could have come from the field's distortion, a result of the weak transmission. It was difficult to say that the two men were identical because of the difference in their clothing, too; Sao was in an elegant, black jacket in this world, while he dressed in worn short sleeves in the other. He had a different hairdo too.

Despite the hardship in identifying the man, eventually it was obvious that both of them were Sao. Those three in the other universe were already speaking about something, so detective Fincher said:

"Mr. Weakman, would you turn on the audio, please?" and Mr. Weakman was kind enough to do so.

". . . I said I've had enough!" bellowed Jack, turning to the woman with Asian features. "I don't really care if you say that he is my son and you're in need, I don't care about anything or anybody!" shouted Jack, while another groan passed though the guests in this living room. This was the favourite way to express dismay among them. From this fraction of discussion, they had already seen the case proven—that Sao was definitely Jack's son in this world too—but detective Fincher gestured for silence.

"I know you don't care, but you should've thought about that when you gave your sperm to the genetic bank in Hanoi. You got one-time payment for your donation. In the document you signed, there was a disclosure—your name can be given to the mother who can demand for support."

"Bullshit!" shouted Jack. "There was no document to sign. There was a war, and we all fought for the liberty of Asia! For you!"

The mourners started to whisper about the second Asian Conflict—resulting in New-China's expansion—finished with a swift peace treaty twelve years ago.

"Then what is this?" the woman standing in the other world waved a paper in front of Jack's nose. Mr. Weakman was kind enough to zoom in on the text so everybody could see Jack's signature and the title: *Declaration of Paternity*.

"The government asked me to compensate the losses," said Jack. "Asia was in agony, so every second soldier helped in the re-creation process. So you all go and milk every one of us?"

"I don't know what the others do," said the woman quietly, "I just want to send my son to university. I don't want anything more. You got *premium* money for your sperm. If you need that money, why did you give permission for them to share your name?"

"It was only enough to buy this shithole. It's a run-down, deserted house with only one room I can use. The roof over the bedroom has leaks, it's full of mildew, and not to mention the ramshackle kitchen. So all that premium money went to this! Where do you want me to get money for you? From the dirt-cheap veteran pension I get?" asked Jack and left the blue jelly bubble, walking towards the bedroom. The woman and the young man who looked like Sao stayed in the living room.

"OK, but what the heck does this prove?" said the widow, sitting on the elbow rest of the couch. She stood up and walked into the bubble with ease. It looked like she wasn't as scared as the rest of the group, who were even frightened to touch the substance. Or she didn't have anything to lose.

"Here is that man, looking like Sao, and the Asian woman—but how does it connect to our world?" she asked with an insolent look. "Why would it happen the same way there as it has here? Jack is alive there, but here you can find only his atoms diffused into the world. What do you want to conclude from this?"

"Mrs. Spencer, please sit back down, I'll try to explain everything," Mr. Fincher told her politely, and the woman complied uncomfortably with his request. "As you can see, your husband is a military veteran in the *other* universe too. He fought in the Asian Conflict—according to the picture we have on the wall of his living room. With many of his fellow heroes, he restored the peace in that continent and stopped the escalation of the crisis to a bigger—potentially worldwide—war. But the most important fact: he had a descendant through the sample he gave to a sperm bank. Due to this information, I have to ask you: was Jack drafted by the military twenty five years ago? If yes, could this gentleman standing here, Mr. Sao, be his son?"

"How the hell should I know? I've only been his wife for five years. But if something happened in the other realm, it doesn't necessarily mean it happened here," said the widow with her arm outstretched.

The discussion came to an end in this world, because the other Jack came back from the bedroom with a small box in his hand.

"Look, this is all I have," he said to the woman, giving her a box covered with black silk. "This is an engagement ring that I wanted to give to a very kind woman who could possibly change my life. Apart from this, I can give you my military medals, but they're worth nothing," he told the truth, because the Cross of Courage, which was also a prestigious military decoration in this world, was hanging on the wall of the other living room.

Some of the guests in the present realm remarked how little the other Jack had in his alternate world.

The woman put the ring into her handbag without a word. The man resembling Sao straightened his hand for a half-hearted handshake, and then both of them disappeared from sight. Jack came back a few minutes later and collapsed into the chair. Some blisters on his face were already opened, leaking a mixture of blood and pus down his chin to his neck. Many of the guests covered their eyes. They did not look as the man cleaned the wounds with a pipette, dropping presumably some kind of medication onto them. It was really a disgusting thing to watch.

As he finished, he looked at his watch and jumped from the chair. In the realm of the investigation, it was eight o'clock, so it had gotten dark already. Mr. Fincher explained to the group that the time was not inevitably the same as in the other world. Most of them had no clue what to expect in this situation, not to mention the existence of a parallel universe in the first place.

But everybody jumped away in this living room when Jack stepped next to the sofa, and changed it into a double bed by pulling the extension out from below. He put clean sheets on before he left for the bathroom. A few minutes later, he came back in his bathrobe, holding a perfume bottle and a piece of cloth, which he used to make his blisters more acceptable. Sometimes Jack's face turned to a painful grimace when the fragrant liquid went deeply into the fresh wounds. Finally, he stuck bandages on them. The relatives and guests whispered again—some said the perfume was for disinfection only, others said he was waiting for somebody—what other reason was there to be fragrant for the night?

And indeed—suddenly the doorbell rang from the hallway. Somebody opened the door in this universe, because the sound was so realistic, but, of course, there was nobody in front of the door here.

Jack Spencer left the bubble, but Mr. Weakman did not think it important to follow him in this case. Excited chatter started among the guests; who could the visitor be this time?

A woman ran into the scene in a flash, pulling Jack behind her. They intertwined in the middle, Jack holding her passionately while the woman started to open Jack's bathrobe. The woman was dressed like a prostitute—her miniskirt was so short that everything could be seen below, her legs were covered with lace stockings and knee-high lacquer boots. She was pulling the robe with slow, sensual movements down from Jack's shoulder, which made it clear what would happen here in a few minutes.

Many of the guests started to move towards the door—mostly those with teenagers or the older people in the group, whose pulses had spiked with the recent events. The number of mourners was cut in half for now. Only the hard-core stayed, those who wanted to see what would happen with the other Jack or wanted to know the resolution of the present death case. Some changed their positions to get close to the bed to have a better—and perverse—viewpoint of the coming events.

At the next moment, excited sounds filled both living rooms, some guests screamed loudly.

Those who did not watch the events might have thought that everybody got excited when Jack's bathrobe finally fell down to the floor, but that wasn't the reason. The woman stopped kissing Jack at his waistline and pulled back a bit. Her face was clearly recognisable—she was Mary Spencer. Mary, as a professional prostitute, was doing foreplay with her husband who had just died in this world. These bizarre events could only be directed in a movie, but this was the shocking truth of the other reality.

"Mr. Weakman, please turn off the picture and the sound," intervened Detective Fincher. "We are not interested in seeing these events any further. Please record everything and come back when the scene is ready for public view."

Mr. Weakman, as always, knew his task. The blue jelly did not disappear completely, it shrank into a small blob, floating softly one and a half meters high in the middle of the living room—held in standby.

Mary Spencer sat apathetically on the corner of the sofa. Everybody was staring at her, but she avoided eye contact. Detective Fincher broke the silence, "Madame Spencer, what did you feel while you were watching the scenes?"

Mary looked at him dumbfounded.

"What the hell do you think I felt? How would you feel if you were an 'escort service' for somebody?" she asked furiously, showing the quotation marks with her fingers when pronouncing the incriminated words. "What do you think I am? A playmate?"

Among the spectators, there were two people (not including Sao) who thought that's exactly what she was.

"Madame Spencer, I have to ask again: what did you do before you met your late husband, Jack Spencer?"

"What kind of stupid question is that? I was a wealthy woman retired from the business."

"Weren't you a retired widow?"

"I said retired businesswoman, you . . ." Mary just stopped herself from swearing.

"What did you do before your previous husband died, Madame Spencer?" asked the detective, raising his voice. The relatives and guests broke into an excited murmur as they realized that Mary had a husband before Jack.

"I was always a businesswoman, please give me some respect!" shouted the widow in a fury.

"And before those two other marriages—when you became widow as well—what did you do before?"

The room was upside down now, like a courtroom during an indictment—the guests became overexcited. Mary was speechless; she looked into the detective's eyes with rage.

"Mr. Weakman, please show the preselected photos to us," said Mr. Fincher to his technician.

"Here you can see Madame Spencer (at that time her name was Sheila Stratovska) while the police patrol collected her from an illegal whorehouse. She resisted the arrest, was violent with the officers, and drugs were found in her blood. Of course you've changed a lot since then, as a widow of four husbands and a successful businesswoman, haven't you, Madame Spencer?"

"Bastard," muttered Mary, who had played the part of an uncorrupted, dazzling-blonde businesswoman until then. "You cannot do this unpunished."

The time had come for Bill, the neighbour, and for Tim Carlson, the grocer, to leave the house. Probably their consciences woke up at the same time or they felt ashamed—they realised what kind of partner they had.

"Mr. Fincher, I think we can connect back again . . ."

"Yes, Mr. Weakman, please do that."

The small blue bubble slowly filled the room again. Jack and Mary in the other world were sitting on the edge of their bed. Apparently, they'd just finished having sex—Mary was pulling her stockings back on, and Jack lit a cigarette. The sheet was creased around them.

"Why are you sad, honey-bunny?" asked Mary. Her style was completely different from the one in this world, although the image of a virtuous businesswoman faded as the truth was revealed. "Wasn't it as good as last week?"

The man didn't say anything, just blew the smoke in front of him. Mary, half naked, jumped into his lap.

"Don't be so down, honey-bunny! I'll come every week, like I promised."

"I can't pay today..."

She pushed him back suddenly and Jack fell on his back into the quilts.

"Why? What did you do with my usual money? Did you gamble again?"

"I bought you a ring," said Jack calmly and dispassionately. He lay on his back and puffed the smoke to the ceiling.

"Oh yeah?" said Mary, softening and kneeling in front of the man. "Then show it to me!"

Jack inhaled the smoke very slowly to play for time.

"I gave it to somebody. I don't have that anymore."

Mary in the parallel universe jumped hysterically like she'd stepped onto an ember. Many of the remaining guests recoiled in this realm.

"Then why did you tell me? How long have you been playing this game with me? You've fed me with promises for months. I've supplied you with this medication for your Asian disease from that moment to save your face from disintegration," said Mary and placed a long vial on the table.

The small glass vial was combined with a pipette. Jack stubbed out the cigarette with a bored face and pointed to the vial. "So you're saying that's a medication?" he smiled ironically. "You think I don't know what that is? It is the slowest and deadliest killer of all poisons, the extract of the strongest Kayuka mushrooms, which absorb into the skin. An aphrodisiac and drug at the same time. When I drop it onto my blisters I won't be healthier or more beautiful, but I don't care, as all my pain goes away. I don't give a shit that I'll die soon and my body will give up the fight against the poison. I went into this game for you and for the small drops of joy you gave me. What else can I lose?"

The dedicated and compassionate audience roared as one. Interestingly, the Kayuka was a well-known drug in this world too. It was hard to buy and was very expensive.

In the middle of the blue bubble, the other Mary adjusted the silk rose on her stocking, pulled out the pipette from the vial, and suddenly poured the vial's contents—approximately five drops—onto Jack's face.

"Then die of the intoxication, you idiot," she shouted to Jack and threw the vial onto the table. She rushed towards the entrance and Mr. Weakman thought it necessary to follow her this time. The people on this side of the world stood alongside the wall to leave more space for the enlarging blue blob.

Then, suddenly, the front door flew through the scene and landed on the edge of the jelly. Mary lost her balance. Black-clad members of Special Police Force swarmed through the living room in the parallel universe. One of them ordered Mary to put her hands back, while she was handcuffed. Everything happened so quickly that there was no time to be frightened on this side of the realm. Here there was nothing, just dead silence, but continued orders and footsteps came from the other side.

A man wearing a white cloak stepped into the scene. He walked to the table and picked up the vial, placing it into a plastic-bag labelled "evidence". Another white-cloaked man stepped over to Jack with a syringe in his hand.

"The antidote, sir. Don't worry, you will be better in a few days," he told Jack, but his face still held the same glazed, bored look as a few moment before, when Mary poured the poison onto his face.

At that moment in the other realm, an elegant man dressed in a fine, black suit came into the living room from the street. All the mourners who had followed the series of strange incidents reacted with deep dismay; a few hisses came from the background. The exact copy of Detective Fincher stood—in full life size—in the parallel living room.

"Sheila Stratovska, I arrest you for the charge of premeditated attempted murder against Mr. Jack Spencer. I also charge you with four other premeditated murders you committed against your previous clients. We know about the poison and we have your fingerprints, so society will get rid of you for a long while. Take her!"

The black-clad unit took the woman out of the scene, and Jack had been escorted to an ambulance too. One white-cloaked man stayed in the blue blob and started to pack his forensic equipment. Before he left, Mr. Fincher turned to him, "Mr. Weakman, would you give me the vial, please?"

The audience in this world had just realised that this man was the real alter ego of Mr. Weakman—sitting behind his miraculous equipment. The brave ones, who stayed behind for the final events, looked at each other for an explanation, desperate and feeling that they'd totally lost the plot.

The technician gave the plastic bag to the detective and left the house into the street of the other realm—everybody could hear the sound of the closing door from this side. Detective Fincher stood in the other living room with the bag in his hand. Cautiously, he took a rubber glove and examined the vial. He held it up against the faint light from the ceiling lamp. It seemed he was looking for something.

"It's only one drop, exactly one drop left. That's what we need."

He pushed the pipette to its place to seal the vial and carefully positioned it in the middle of the table—checking if it stood still. He took off the gloves, strictly folded and pocketed them, then looked around before he left.

"It's all yours," he said waving to the empty room. After he closed the door, the living room appeared empty in the other universe.

It was the most bizarre sentence of all that the guests had heard in the past hour. It looked like magic, like all of them were under the influence of Kayuka's poison and having a delirious trip there. None of them said anything, just looked eagerly at Detective Fincher, because he was the only person to whom the other Mr. Fincher could be talking.

"Mr. Weakman, would you adjust the focus, please?"

The bubble shrunk again. It stopped where the vial stood on the table, gently surrounding it with vivid blue light.

"Madame Spencer, I arrest you by the authority of the State of California with the charge of killing Mr. Jack Spencer. I also charge you with the premeditated murder of your three previous husbands. Please stand up and come with me to the police station. I hope I won't need to use force against you."

The woman jumped off the sofa.

"What do you think you're doing? What kind of evidence do you have? All of my husbands died in the hospital! You think this little game you played here, and the alleged crime in the parallel universe, this little vial . . ." said Mary and, with a high swing, she grabbed the evidence in the middle of the table. She was shocked when it stayed in her hand.

Another murmur—the biggest of that afternoon—ran through the audience.

"You just got it, Madame Spencer. You gave us the perfect evidence. This vial looks like the ones we've found in the backyard of your previous houses—unfortunately, all were cleaned, polished, and without fingerprints. On this—unfortunately—we have your fingerprints already, so we can put you in jail."

"You filthy little . . ." Mary shouted and jumped on the detective. Fincher easily shook her off and handcuffed her. The lustrous dame from before now looked like an insane prostitute.

"You rotten bastard," she shouted towards Sao, "you said you would never inform the police! You scammed me, telling me we'd do everything and share together, go to hell!"

"Take her into the car," said Fincher to the member of the Special Force Unit who came into the house for the final act. "Mr. Weakman, I would like to thank you for your outstanding work and expertise."

He put the vial back into the plastic bag and slid it into his pocket. Mr. Weakman closed the collapsible table while others started to move towards the exit.

*

Detective Fincher approached his skycar when Reverend Delgado stepped next to him.

"Mr. Fincher, may I stop you for a few words?"

The detective saw that the reverend was heavily confused and under the influence of what had just happened in the house.

"Of course, Reverend Delgado, I'll listen to you."

"May I ask you, how did you know? How did you know that Mary committed the exact same crime in the parallel universe?"

Fincher was continuously smiling while he looked at him.

"I didn't know. I just hoped that we would have a desirable result. Nothing can be predicted in the parallel worlds."

"But here . . . in this world . . . will Sao be the heir? Do you have the solid evidence that he is Jack's son?" asked Reverend Delgado, pointing to Sao, who was about to get into the car next to Mr. Weakman.

"Do you mean Agent Lee? No, he just played the role. We had to use bait to catch the big fish, don't you think?"

"But he was there in the parallel universe, together with his mother..."

Detective Fincher lowered the window of the police car, which was already floating above the road. He patted the reverend's arm in a friendly gesture.

"You don't always need to believe what you see."

"But that vial..."

Fincher straightened his arm for a handshake.

"C'mon, Reverend, do you really believe in parallel worlds?" he asked finally, and accelerated. The police car, bathed in orange-blue light, climbed towards to the LA skyways and left the reverend with doubts floating in the air.

I don't believe in them, thought the reverend, *I'll stay with my own beliefs.*

He turned back and went to the nearest skytaxi-station.

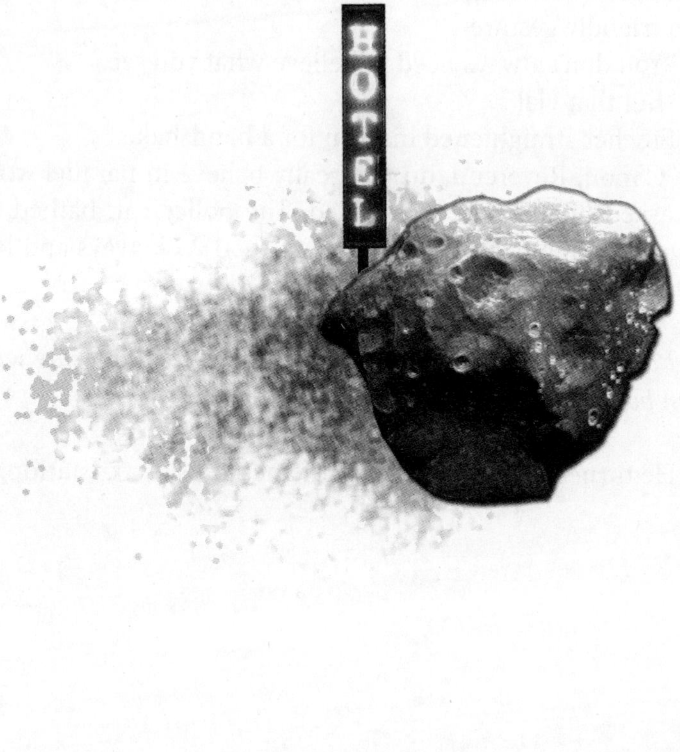
HOTEL

VII.

Doomsday, 2241

Rupert could not sit still. His father, Charlie, had asked him a million times to sit back but without result. The kid was hyperactive.

"I want to look out the window!" he shouted when Charlie pushed him gently back to his place.

"You're not allowed to leave your seat before we reach orbit, so please stay calm! You see that angry-eyed man watching you from there? He will come here and throw you out to space!"

It was true, what Charlie said: the flight attendant was keeping an eye on the boy. He raised his hand, forming a pistol with his fingers, and targeted Rupert. The boy became frightened and descended back into his chair. He had even fastened his seatbelt, though he'd complained earlier that it was too tight for him. He probably thought that all naughty kids would be thrown out and would orbit forever around the Earth.

Charlie could finally relax. All his muscles were tense from the fight he'd had with Rupert. He shouldn't have brought the kid with him, but he wasn't comfortable leaving him with the babysitter. The upcoming events and the news frightened him—although he was a scientist himself. All those horrific end-of-the-world scenarios rang in his ear like a never-ending echo.

"You shouldn't frighten him so much," said the woman sitting next to them. "This hysteria with the doomsday is plenty for us!"

The fellow traveller was pretty, without wrinkles, although she must have been well over sixty. Her long hair was held together by a net.

"I don't think we're in serious danger, despite what the media's ululating suggests. You can believe me, everything—even the unexpected events—can be solved with the techniques we have nowadays," explained Charlie, almost to himself, as the woman did not appear so anxious.

"You're right, there are some people who want to generate hysteria, although the travel agencies and the Fleet are working hard to avoid all complications," said the woman and gently put her hands on Charlie's arm. "Don't you work for the Fleet? I love those handsome astronauts so much!" she exclaimed with a wide smile. There was a real man-eater diva behind the genetically engineered beauty.

"No," countered Charlie immediately. "My wife, Sarah, is on that ship, you may be able to see on your side. There's a big, bright blue star on its side. It's the Fleet fastest ship. So we just got a VIP ticket to this parabolic flight to see these major events."

"Oh, that's wonderful! Don't worry about those jinxes who say this will be the last day of the Earth. This asteroid had a close approach to our planet sixty-three times in the last century, I don't believe it will cause problems now," said the diva, waving while she searched for the ship with the blue star.

"It's not a problem with the asteroid itself," said Charlie, shaking his head. "The Laius asteroid is not hazardous for the Earth. The real danger lies in those private space agencies and their increasingly absurd ideas. We can't trust them anymore, as they want to milk out the last new-dollars from these flying rocks," said Charlie, but the woman wasn't listening to him anymore, she let out a high scream when she'd found the ship.

"Yes, I've found it! It's gorgeous! You must have had an adroit wife if she's on that!"

"Yes, she's the first officer. She always wanted to fly, even as a kid. So we became the earth-bound boys, am I right, Rupert?" he asked his son, caressing his hair. But Rupert was still fixated on the angry-eyed man, waiting for the moment when he would stand up and relegate all boys to the coldness of space.

"One of my husbands was a soldier," said the diva, straightening her back. "He was tall and handsome; he looked marvellous in his uniform. But I didn't like the long-distance relationship. When he was relocated to Mars New Home, I decided to divorce. Although he was the finest man I've ever had!" finished the diva with a pose—when she clasped her fingers together, she looked more like a granny, but her face and body remained young like a fresh spring sprout.

"But I've met my real love now, after so many years!" *and after so many digested husbands,* thought Charlie, while the woman was running through her motions. "He is a real adventurer. I'm going to see him—or I would say I'll be his fellow adventurer—on his trip. It is so unbelievable, what I'm doing for love!" she said, giggling like a girl.

The spacejet finally reached the top of the orbit and the signal for the seatbelts went out. Rupert didn't have the guts to move, he was constantly watching for the flight attendant to disappear behind the door. When the angry-eyed attendant left, he squinted to his father to find out what would happen next. He was still bound by the notion of ice-cold space.

"OK, cowboy, you can go. The Indians aren't in town anymore," said Charlie, then Rupert shot into the air like a bullet. In the weak artificial gravity, it was easy to climb to the round windows. He started to smash the glass with his toy ship.

"There is Mammy, there is Mammy!" He shouted towards the cruiser, which entered the dark, shadowy sickle of the Earth like a bright needle.

"So you're going for the long trip? Did you buy a ticket?" asked Charlie, surprised, turning back to their fellow traveller.

"I haven't paid for just one trip, my dear; I've joined for a lifetime! I bought an apartment!" said the woman, raising her head proudly. "My knight, my lover, has already moved into it and is waiting for me. He said he couldn't afford a place like that, but if I bought one, he'd happily move in with me. How wonderful it is!"

"Yes, it is wonderful, if we survive the day," added Charlie, smiling. No matter how much he trusted the Fleet and his wife, the possibility was still running through his head. It must have been that strange misgiving—generated by the news channels—that was constantly buzzing in his mind.

"Look, other ships are arriving!" the diva broke into excitement. "They're taking it very seriously. I hope they don't think this rock will hit the Earth this time. I think they've exaggerated the preparation a bit."

Two other ships were lined up on the orbit, closer to the Moon, opposite Sarah's ship, the Midnight Star. The three ships took up a triangular position to better control the area in case they needed to use their weapons.

"Look, Daddy, lots of ships standing there!" shouted Rupert from above, where he could see the armada. A sea of private or corporate-owned spaceships or spacejets on which thousands of people wanted to witness the Laius's arrival—*or to flee from Earth in case something disastrous happens*, thought Charlie.

There had been a massive wave of panic on the Earth when they announced the new arrival of the asteroid—the size of twenty football fields. According to the latest calculation, it would fly closer than the nearest satellite's orbit. A few million tons of old space junk floated at that level, which could modify the speed and the trajectory of the Laius.

But this is why we're using the Fleet, Charlie told himself, *to clean the crossroad in space.*

The private space agencies obviously grabbed the opportunity to sell all the tickets on every available ship they had. Everything was fully booked. Even companies operating cargo ships changed their fleet to host space tourists; they reconstructed the big container freighters to serve as lookout stations. One company used inflatable lookout capsules; hundreds of them were floating on the horizon like a string of beads.

But many people didn't believe the Fleet could keep the asteroid under control. That's why so many bought space emergency shelters. These were fully equipped orbiters that could hold complete families. The manufacturer guaranteed these self-sustainable units—with enough drinking water and edible protein for four people—for forty-three years. They calculated this warranty time based on the estimated time it would take authorities to restore the situation on Earth after the fragments of the asteroid—blown up by the Fleet—hit the surface. Then the dust would settle, and life would be restored. These shelters were too expensive for most people, but they still sold well—they quickly became in short supply. The waiting list was so long, and the panic brought up a new industry. Those who felt themselves in real danger left the Earth; they relocated to the Moon, Europa, or Mars New Home Colony. Although, the average person just bought a ticket to one of the panorama ships and hoped for a positive outcome.

"Ladies and Gentlemen, I would ask those passengers who are going with the transfer to the Oedipus Module to please wait in the hall in front of the docking tube," communicated the *angry-eyed* flight attendant who'd made Rupert behave like an angel. Charlie couldn't stand without laughing while he caressed his son's head.

"My time has come! My darling is waiting for me," the diva said gladly and picked up her tiny handbag. "My keys are in here," she said proudly, caressing the leather bag. "And he's waiting for me up there in the lounge of the Oedipus Module. He's been living there already for fourteen years, and he's never seen a woman like me before. We'll have an outstanding life, wandering through space, between the stars . . ." she was obviously exaggerating—this was her annoying style—because the Oedipus wasn't going to outer space. It would stay in the solar system to go on its turns around the sun.

"Daddy, are we going too?" asked Rupert, pointing to the leaving passengers.

"No, unfortunately not, my dear. We're staying. Mammy would be so sad if we disappeared for fourteen years. You would cry if she couldn't tell you a bedtime story by next week."

A wave of passengers flowed towards to the exit. Charlie thought he would never leave the Earth for that desolate rock. He was sure that most of the ingoing chose the Oedipus due to the global hysteria. In case of any complications, the module could move away from the Earth. It had enough supplies for twenty years. After fourteen years, when it came near the planet again, they could get off and evaluate the damage on Earth.

"See you, my dears!" said the diva, screaming with excitement. "Love and star travel are waiting for me! Enjoy the show!"

She slowly—and finally—dissolved into the crowd. Charlie and Rupert were the only ones left. They'd gotten their tickets for the entertainment only.

"Mr. Simpson?" The angry-eyed flight attendant stepped next to them. Rupert immediately hid behind his father. "The captain would like to invite you to the bridge, where you can follow the arrival more comfortably," he said, smiling, and there was a lollipop in his hand. Rupert squinted out from his hiding place above Charlie's shoulder. He did not come out, but quickly straightened his hand to catch the sweet—like the moray when it shoots out from its cave—and run towards the door. They didn't catch up to him until the stairs leading to the upper deck.

The bridge was huge compared to the size of the ship. They could look through the large panoramic windows while they sat in comfortable, padded seats right behind the crew. The Angry Eyes brought some refreshments. Rupert showed the little toy ship to him, so the previous tension dissolved as they played their game together.

The Laius was already visible on the large screens.

The Catapult Space Agency, which had financed the Oedipus Project, transmitted the lives pictures from their spaceships. The agency had been following the Laius Complex—which contained the Laius asteroid and the connected Habitat Module, the Oedipus—for two weeks. Charlie was amazed at the sight of the artificial module and the space rock spinning around each other like sublime space dancers. Robots worked around the cables, which connected the module to the asteroid—they had prepared for the separation. Those who had been living on the Oedipus Complex wanted to separate the Habitat from the Laius asteroid—the end-of-the-world hysteria had reached their home too. They felt themselves safer on the near-Earth orbit, and they could reconnect when they passed the home planet.

"We're starting the separation procedure now," said a voice in the mist of the static noise. "Three-two-one . . . and separation. I can confirm; the separation has finished. The Oedipus Module is free. I repeat; the Oedipus is free. You may now begin boarding new passengers."

After this announcement, small space ferries and pods accelerated towards the complex. The diva and others were on their way to their future and happiness. Soon the ferries became small dots and disappeared in the background of the stars.

"Midnight Star calling Spacejet 2; Sarah Richardson, first officer, speaking. May I speak with my family on a separate channel?"

"Of course, First Officer Richardson, I'll connect you to them," said the captain. Rupert's new friend, formerly Angry Eyes, came back with two earpiece communicators in his hand.

"Mammy, you will not believe it, there are so many ships around us!" the boy exclaimed zealously once the communicator got connected. "They look like little ants. I see your ship too. Do you see us? Do you see the toy in my hand? It has the same name as yours!"

"I see, my dear, of course I see," said Sarah smiling from the screen next to them. "I hope you were a good boy and didn't turn the ship upside down!"

Rupert cautiously squinted at his father and hoped he wouldn't mention the plan about exiling him into space.

"It was all seamlessly perfect with the space cowboy," said Charlie, exchanging a meaningful glance with Rupert. "When can we see you in person?"

"If all goes as planned, I'll be home in twelve hours," said Sarah, making a strange grimace. Charlie noticed this.

"Why? Did you hear something troubling?" asked Charlie, while he took away Rupert's earpiece. The boy didn't need to know about serious matters.

"I don't know, the calculated data coming from our tactical computers is not so promising. The Laius is approaching at a thirty-degree angle to the plane of the solar system. If you look now to your upper left side, you will see it."

Indeed, there was a small, bright point—one-tenth the size of the Moon—above the Earth.

"According to the new calculations," she added again, "the separation has changed the course of the object. Because of its non-symmetrical shape, the Laius asteroid could even touch the upper airspace of the Earth. I am not at all relaxed. The Catapult Agency said that their special ships, the pushers, are ready to intervene at any moment."

" I think that, as Catapult's leader, Panič has gone too far for the sake of his profits this time. The Fleet shouldn't have let it happen" said Charlie, clenching the armrest in anger.

"You can be sure we're ready for everything. We can shoot that rock into small fragments together with the Oedipus Module if needed. Can you imagine how much families have spent globally for evacuation and shelters? We should've blown up this ugly rock far from the Earth instead . . ."

"The corporate colonial law is protecting them, you can't do that," said Charlie. "Laius is the property of the Catapult Consortium. Until they're putting people in danger, you can't intervene."

"We'll see. I think they will do everything to keep the rock on track. I have to finish now," said Sarah, sighing. "If all goes well, I'll have a surprise for you boys!"

"OK, honey, we'll wait for the surprise. Whatever happens, I love you!" said Charlie and touched the screen at the place where Sarah's face was.

"I love you both," waved Sarah on the fading picture.

Such a brave woman, but still so affectionate, Charlie thought. It had made for a successful marriage—no matter what happened in the next few minutes.

"The *pushers* are ready," said the voice from the operation room. "Flyby in twelve minutes. According to the newest calculation, we need to adjust four degrees on the track to avoid collision."

The middle field of view became empty. The ships, filled with spectators, retracted into further position. Based on the new calculation, there was no doubt anymore which part of the orbit needed to be empty.

What an interesting creature the human is, thought Charlie, *how he fears losing his life, but will be a catastrophe-tourist when he smells danger.* Man also liked to play with fire and to feel the rush of adrenaline in the blood. He was a fear maniac, and this fear awakened his ancient survival instincts. Despite this, mankind made dangerous plans. They kept an enormous asteroid on near-Earth orbit in order to have bigger profits and satisfaction, risking other people's lives, people who were not happy with the fear and adrenaline rush. Terrible and magnificent the human is. His soul is free but sometimes he pushes so far . . .

"Flyby in seven minutes. *Pushers* are in line. We're correcting course now!" the distant voice in the Catapult Operational Center had given the order. The continuously growing rock was already bigger than the Moon, covering a big part of the starry background. Above the Laius was the teardrop-shaped Oedipus Module with its shiny surface reflecting the sunlight. Bright, needle-sharp blue lights came out of the *pushers'* steering nozzle when they made the asteroid's corrective manoeuvre. The rock went into a slow, barely visible spin.

"Start the automatic transmission for the news, now!" The well-known face of Slobodan Panič, the Serbian multimillionaire, appeared on the screen. The fifty-year-old space-businessman was standing in front of the Consortium's building with a huge statue—forming a Catapult—behind him. In his hand there was the model of the Laius Complex—the asteroid Laius and the Oedipus Module connected together.

"Welcome, everybody around the globe," he started his pre-recorded speech, "my name is Slobodan Panič, the chairman and owner of the Catapult Consortium. Today we witness a big event in our lives; after fourteen years of successful operations, we have new inhabitants coming to our module. I would like to thank all of you who helped in this big achievement: colleagues, partners, and mostly for those who have been working for the module's maintenance and service, flying connected to Laius in the past years. We've had some wonderful events in the past; the flybys at Uranus and Saturn; we (faithful to our name) used the gravitational catapult effect of the gas giant, Jupiter. And now we're at near-Earth orbit to show the Mother Colony—for the future passengers, for you—how magnificent this Complex is. I've gotten a lot of criticism in the past, accusations that I've put humankind in danger of extinction by capturing the Laius. But let me draw your attention to those hundreds of pioneering inventions that we've created through this project; the pushers, those little ships working around the asteroid right now, which can be used to divert dangerous objects from a collision course. And I'll mention the self-sufficient life support systems, which are..."

"Firework cartridges, on my mark. Now!" said the earlier voice from the Operational Center from a separate speaker. The Laius was very close now, Rupert wanted to catch it through the window, but it was already twice the size of his palm. Suddenly, lights came into life on the dark side of the asteroid; the cartridges formed an enormous ad—*Catapult into the happiness*. It was truly impressive.

But the next moment, the alarm went off, bathing the whole ship in red.

"The present track is too close to the collision course," they could hear the sharp voice from the speakers. "The *pushers* are at maximum. Mayday!"

Rupert sat back in his chair and squeezed his father's hand. Charlie embraced him, but he worried more for Sarah and the other twenty-eight billion people on the Earth.

The Laius ran through the scene like the large load of the catapult. Its speed was twenty-two thousand kilometers per hour, the highest among the space-wanderers discovered in the last century. It was beginning to eclipse the sun as it reached the plane of the Earth's orbit.

The rock did not change its course, although the *pushers*' engines were continuously belching the energy beams.

"Thrust to the maximum on every engine," came the order from Operation.

"I am on maximum on both nozzles, but the gravity is more powerful!" said one pilot from the pusher, struggling to gain more power from the machine.

While the Laius was rotating, it went into the upper part of the Earth's stratosphere with its sharp, salient edges. It cut through the air like a blade into a pillowcase, and it made a long, white-hot line with cloud patches as if they were floating feathers. Between the bright, fiery clouds and the planet's surface, there was tons of dust and debris. The waves of fragments reached them too—the small pieces of rocks hit the windows and sounded like hail on a tin roof.

The sudden voice of Captain Simo Bushido—who was Sarah's superior—broke through the air:

"If it continues to spin like this, the thick air will pull the asteroid into the stratosphere. Midnight Star—ready all weapons. On my mark, we fire at the asteroid. The aim is to cut it into pieces and reduce the possible impact weight and damage."

So it is happening, thought Charlie. The doomsday had finally arrived because of one man's greed.

"I can't hold my position," shouted the *pusher's* pilot in a horrified voice. Charlie covered Rupert's ears. "I've lost the heat shield! The *pushers* aren't designed for these, I don't know how long..."

His voice faded into static noise and finally dissolved in the fireball that appeared on the side of the Laius—the pusher vanished into the stratosphere. The explosion started a chain reaction, tearing off more salient edges from the asteroid and pushing big clouds of debris towards the surface. The pieces descended into the deeper atmosphere with large smoky tails behind them.

"Operation, be ready for collision of small and medium-sized debris," it was the firm voice of Captain Bushido again. "Catapult Operation, this is the Midnight Star. I'm taking over control of the operation under the authorization of the United Colony Council. Withdraw the remaining *pushers* and prepare the passengers and the crew of the Oedipus Module for the nearby explosion. We open fire on Laius in one minute."

"You can't do that. The Laius is private property," disagreed the controller at the Catapult Consortium.

"The authority was signed by the UCC Security Council and countersigned by your boss, Mr. Panič. You still have forty-five seconds to finish the necessary procedures."

At that moment, something bizarre happened. The Oedipus Module overtook the spinning asteroid, which had been slowed down by the friction resistance. It nicely positioned itself in the line of fire between the Laius and the Midnight Star. Charlie thought about Sarah's sentence: *we can shoot that rock into small fragments together with the Oedipus Module if needed.*

"Ready to fire!" Bushido's voice was determined, like his Samurai's ancestors.

The Laius burned on the edge of the upper stratosphere. Its spin slowed down as it floated on the top of the thin air, like a pebble thrown on the surface of the water.

"Object in the line of fire," Sarah gave this status report. "Don't give the order yet."

"All right, but if the module does not move out, we have been authorized to shoot it down too. Ready for double fire. Twenty seconds."

It was a horrible twenty seconds. Charlie pulled Rupert onto his lap, and they held each other so tightly that they started to sweat. *What horror must the passengers be experiencing now on the Oedipus Module?* thought Charlie. Would they be casualties to save the other billions on the Earth?

"Weapon preparedness goes back to normal," said Captain Bushido firmly when the Laius finally slid down from the Earth's upper stratosphere. Its shape changed radically, it lost its salient edges and became rounded by the friction resistance where it came into contact with the air.

"Catapult Operation to the Fleet, thank you for the help. We will estimate the damages and check if we can connect the cables from the *Oedipus* Module to the *Laius*."

"Negative, Catapult Operation," opposed Captain Bushido with a peremptory tone in his voice. "You lost all rights to decide on the future of Laius based on the safety clause: 'If the private investor does not apply maximum care and the project causes global danger on Earth or another Colony, the Fleet will take control over Complex until . . .'"

"Captain Bushido, if you'll let me say a word . . ." it was Panič himself. "As you can see, there is no danger anymore. The

Laius is heading to the far, empty part of the solar system. The Oedipus Module has no major damage, so it's ready to continue its operation. In this case, you don't need to maintain command any longer."

"Do you really think so, Mr. Panič?" asked Bushido with slight sarcasm. "According to the tactical computer, the course of the asteroid changed the wrong way, which means for the next rendezvous we have an 87% chance of hitting the Earth. Your pushers scored badly on the test and you lost one of your colleagues. The Oedipus Module is drifting in space without control, its course will intersect the trajectory of the Laius in forty minutes—the collision is inevitable. Two of the tie-down points have been damaged, and the available two are not sufficient to tie the module safely. We've received a private transmission from the module, I will play it back to you."

"Please help us!" a desperate woman screamed on the recording, the sounds of intense chaos filling the background. "We want to be evacuated right now!"

Bushido was waiting for Panič to react, but there was no word from the other side, only the dim sound of his breath could be heard.

"I know that you blocked all outgoing calls from the Oedipus to hide the situation there," continued the captain of the Midnight Star, "but we have the necessary equipment to connect the phones from a distance."

He held a small pause to let him digest the facts.

"In addition to this, I have to tell you that the debris has reached the surface. If the first, bigger part had hit a town, we might have had millions of casualties, but fortunately it landed in an abandoned area. The second, smaller fragment started a tsunami in the South Pacific, which luckily generated only two-meter-high waves—but may have destroyed many ships on the way through the ocean."

"According to these facts," he continued, "our ship is going after the Oedipus Module and will start the evacuation process. We've already contacted the crew on the module and they've started guiding the passengers towards to the airlocks. After we finish the process, we will blow up the module and the asteroid as well. We'll continue to do this until the fragments reach a harmless size."

When he finished, there was nobody listening on the other side of the line. Panič must have realized that the authorities would charge him with murder due to negligence and endangerment of humankind. He might already have been placed under arrest.

"Lieutenant Richardson, please accelerate to start the evacuation process and prepare the ferries."

"Yes, Captain, heading one-four-two, automatic trajectory tracking. Medical Team, please prepare for the injuries," answered Sarah.

Charlie was so proud of his wife. A few minutes later, her face appeared on the screen next to them.

"Boys, you were so brave!" she said, smiling into the camera. "Unfortunately, I'll have to postpone my surprise, which was a ticket to Moon Colony for a couple of days. Please cross your fingers for me that everything will be alright out here, and I'll see you soon!"

Rupert was already sleeping. Sarah sent a kiss then the line broke off. The long needle-shaped Midnight Star flashed in the sunlight before jumping after the Oedipus Module.

The armada of ships was still standing in front of the bright blue sickle of the Earth, they all must be under the shock of the recent events. Charlie blew out all his worries with a big sigh together with billions of people on the Earth.

*

Hundreds of passengers were treated on the deck of the Midnight Star's Hospital Section on the way back to Earth. Among them, there was a diva sobbing violently. The nurse could not calm her down, only a sedative injection would help her.

"Oh my poor soul! I lost everything!" she cried and buried her face in her hands. She looked like an aging soul enclosed in a young body.

"Please, you can relax now," said the nurse, touching her hand gently. "Think about how many millions have been saved today from a possible catastrophe. The doomsday did not come this time."

"But my beautiful life, my lover, my future! It all went pear-shaped! This is the real doomsday! I knew it would be disastrous for me, because I read somewhere that Oedipus killed his father, Laius! The ancient curse happened again!"

The nurse gently covered her with a soft blanket and thought that the end of the world was a relative concept that could be different to each individual. For her, the doomsday had not yet arrived, because her family was waiting for her back on Earth.

She cheered up just thinking about them.

WE NEED

M.O.R.E.

VIII.

The van der Bruck Incident

His long hair was floating around him in the weightless interior of the cabin like seaweed—or like elephant grass in a storm, as he'd seen ages ago on an ancient documentary. Strange, that he was thinking about that . . . right now. He could not move his hands, they were handcuffed to the two side of the rounded window. They wanted him to see all along, minute by minute. This was part of his punishment. As he was falling into the void . . .

*

They'd landed two days ago with a scheduled flight to the Europa Colony, separate from the passengers. A complete and heavily equipped army sat in front to guard them. The two men were bound, their legs were tied to the seats and their hands to each other. They bore electronic collars and armlets to make sure they wouldn't even think about escaping. But they were not fit enough for a run—they couldn't even sit up straight against the g-force of the breaking manoeuvre without their necks going numb.

For the last two years they had been transferred from jail to jail—thirty-seven times they'd moved and had to present themselves in front of different courts. Between two verdicts, they were in luxurious circumstances; the prisoners wanted to live as normally as they could until the final verdict. The whole Solar System was following their trial.

There were two of them against the world. *If I'm ever finally free, I'll write a book about it*—thought Peter van der Bruck with a bittersweet smile, when they were led into the armoured police snowflyer. *The van der Bruck Incident That Changed the World*—the title would be something like that, if the news media named them after Peter, The van der Bruck Gang.

If Simon doesn't screw up the whole thing, he thought. His gang mate was sitting not far away in a private cell, behind bulletproof glass. He'd started to howl and whine yesterday, and sometimes shrieked, "They'll hang us all!" Simon Barrens—the Rat, as they called him in the underground world of silicon chips—had never been a strong character. When he joined into a hustle, he was full of wild ideas, but when the wind of legal punishment touched his butt, he became a squealing rat running into a dark corner. He was sitting there like a cornered rodent, with unquenchable fear in his eyes, looking out the window while they passed by the sign of the *Haag District*.

This was the first time Peter had come to Europa, Jupiter's dirty-white moon. The Haag District was the territory of the United Colony Council, with rights to decide in Colonial or International legal cases. It strangely reminded him of his ancestors' birthplace, the Netherlands, especially because of the *Haag District*.

Before he was caught, he'd lived on the Mars Colony. He didn't leave the place for several years, he was hiding. Fifteen years ago, when he'd fled from the Earth, his flight stopped on the Moon Colony to pick up transit passengers. But he wouldn't leave the ship to see the Moon Colony, he felt more secure in the belly of the ship while the crew gathered all transit passengers. He didn't want to risk crossing the border again.

But life here sucked compared to the Martian environment. The cold got deep into the bones despite the polar overalls he had to don each court day. They couldn't increase the surface temperature enough—to be at least liveable—with the geothermic reactors, so the base had to be moved down into the ground.

The snowflyer noiselessly rushed on the several square kilometres thick ice plates, following the path lined by bright lights. Peter stolidly stared at the swirling ice crystals. The skis must like the icy surface, he thought, although they didn't touch the ground much due to the low gravity. On this icy highway, contrary to the base—which connected the spaceport with the Haag District—there was no artificial Earth-type gravity.

After two hours of the monotonous whooshing, they arrived at the block of the courthouse. Everything happened as if it were copied from yesterday. People from the press were pushing and jostling each other for better positions behind the cordon, driving antigrav cameras above them to catch a snapshot of an interesting moment. It would be a good grimace from him, or a desperate, *scared-shitless* moment from Simon. The pictures from yesterday were all around the colony on huge floating screens. Simon, the Rat, was looking piteous although Peter thought the lawyer had equipped them with some good advice. He talked about how to hide the panic, when to speak, and when to shut up.

But it seemed that the Rat would collapse today. He was dancing on the thin borderline of a nervous breakdown, the huge neurotic abyss, and some rocks had already started to shift beneath his feet, rolling down into the deep. The biggest problem was they couldn't talk to each other and make a plan; their lawyers couldn't exchange information between them either. They had been separated well before the police made the arrest—Peter flew to Mars, Simon went to the Moon—and had been total amateurs, failing to make a plan in case of trouble. You can run, you can hide, you can scam the biometric scanners, *you can change your biochip; but one day, they will come for you,* thought Peter.

The crowd's hurricane-like roar slowly faded behind them as they descended on the escalator into the deep belly of the moon. Flashes from automated cameras flying around the pitch-blackness of the entrance illuminated the receding figures in the tunnel. The black-dressed special army did not leave the watching to chance; all two hundred kept eyes on them from the front and behind. They spanned both sides of the narrow corridor leading up to the courtroom.

Here we go with the stupid dressing again, thought Peter; he hated the twenty-minute procedure. His long hair was entangled in the chains connecting the handcuffs, the anklets were sometimes tight depending on which guard fitted it.

The courtroom was as packed as a weekend market. In the lower gallery, there were reporters from colonial newspapers, buzzing like hundreds of bees. Above them, people from major television channels around the Solar System thronged; with remote controllers in their hands, they were trying to guide their tiny, buzzing camera drones. These were operating one and a half metres below ceiling level—but now all of them wanted to come as close as possible to the two criminals. Their practical, fist-sized shields protected them from each other in the crowded courtroom airspace.

Of course, Simon whined again like a cornered dog. Peter could even hear that from a distance in the continuous noise, although there were thirty cupboard-sized policemen between them. So he could not tell him to *pull himself together and be a man, finally* . . . he should have been brave enough before, when all the world was looking for them.

Come hell or high water, I don't care, thought Peter, when the courtroom was finally silenced. The massive metallic door next to the bench slid away, and the leading judge appeared in the doorway with two legal experts from each colony. Six law-educated colleagues from Earth followed them. Fine consignment, a team of star-prosecutors from each corner of the Solar System.

The members of the court sat, the swishing of their long juridical gowns amplified in the sinister silence. A few second later, a red light appeared on the communicator, and the court session started.

"I am Jannet Kristensen, the leading judge appointed by the UCC *Haag District*. Welcome to all of you who came for the court case *Humankind v. van der Bruck Gang* on the thirteenth trial day. We have here the prosecutors representing Humankind from the Colonies and the Earth; we have the accused's lawyers appointed by UCC *Haag District* too. I ask all of you to keep yourselves to the legal oath and be loyal to the Colonial laws. I'll open the session now."

Peter was not an unshakeable person. He felt sick when he saw the people dressed in their long black gowns. Even though he felt some chance with this judge. She had a firm and disciplined glance, but there was something ordinary in her too. The way she handled the gavel—hitting it once to open the session—was so airy. She wore her blonde hair in a bun; she had a pretty face and looked to be about fifty. *Maybe we have a small chance,* thought Peter, *if Simon doesn't mess up the whole thing.* The prosecutor colleagues behind her were not as relaxed as the judge; if the defendants managed to walk away with an easy sentence, it wouldn't be because of them.

"I call the witness of the prosecutor, Mr. Graig Tyler. Mr. Ortega, the witness is yours."

"Thank you, Chief Justice Kristensen," said a tall, black-haired man as he stood. He was Antonio Ortega, Chief of the Prosecutors Board. It was obvious, already on the very first day, that Peter and Simon would be facing the toughest prosecutor of Mother Earth. He left no doubt that he would fight in a smart and well-choreographed way against them as the toreador fought against the bull. At the beginning of the process came the *picadors*, the colonies' smaller prosecutors; they made the accused tired with their questions coming sharp as the pikes. Peter and Simon could cope with them, although their napes were not as wide as a bull's to handle pikes. But his composure was slipping; Peter had become enraged by the last day of the trial, which was the purpose of the process. At the end would come the coup de grace, the deathblow with the small *descabello*, right into the middle of the nape vertebras.

"Mr. Tyler, were you the chief executive of the security company, Premier Shield, sixteen years ago?"

"Yes, your information is correct."

"Can you tell me what your company was doing exactly?"

"Yes, sir," said the stocky man, leaning forward on the witness stand. His handlebar moustache was dancing around his face. He was in an old, earthly suit—it had been a long time since people dressed like this on the colonies—emphasizing his connection to the Mother Colony. "Our company dealt with building and maintaining security systems of high-level international and colonial organizations."

"What kind of security systems do you mean?"

"They were physical and virtual systems."

"Including the network connected to these systems?" asked the attorney.

"Yes, sir, of course," answered the man, nodding enthusiastically. Some of the camera drones—with their sparkling optics—were flying around him. Others followed the steps of the attorney who was walking along the bench.

"The Premier Shield," Mr. Ortega stood in front of the witness stand, "is almost unbreakable . . ."

" . . . but we're already in!" said Simon with that grin on his face, the kind you only see in a mental institute. He was sitting squeezed in his rat hole behind nine monitors and surrounded by a pile of uncountable empty candy wrappers. His brain wouldn't work without the proper amount of sugar. The bluish light cast by the screens made his pale, pockmarked face even more lifeless.

"I said I'll make them naked! I'll push down their trousers and they won't even notice!" he said, laughing hysterically. His dreadlocks whipped around his neck as he shook his head.

"OK, you filthy rat, you did it!" exclaimed Peter behind the other console. "Here's the file, inject it!"

"No, wait, check first to be sure we got the money," Peter could see Simon's lunatic eyes between two screens. *He didn't even have a joint*, thought Peter. The idea of all that money must have liberated huge amounts of endorphins in his brain.

"Bullshit, do what I said. Push the file and get out of it. Don't worry about the money!"

"OK, you're the boss!" said Simon, pushing *Enter*. His nimble fingers ran across the keyboard for another twenty minutes, injecting short codes to hide their intrusion. They couldn't be sure if the camouflaged code would work, they would only know in the coming weeks.

"We'll know soon if the worm has entered the hole," Peter nodded as he threw a beer can onto Simon's lap.

"Jeez, this is cold as hell!" shrieked the Rat. "Right on target . . ."

". . . but I didn't know why I needed to inject the worm-virus," Simon whined. Peter almost jumped but his chains wouldn't let him catch Simon's neck. *This weak guy will collapse*, he thought.

"What exactly was the program inside the worm?" asked the attorney, fixing his eyes on his floundering victim. Simon was practically curled into a foetal position.

"I programmed it to prepare the way for a bigger piece of software," answered Simon, looking for help in his lawyer's eye. The lawyer shook his head, confused. *He's going to say too much*, thought Peter, annoyed.

"You call this short code a nest in that special IT world where you work, don't you?" The attorney seemed prepared, even knowing hackers' jargon.

"Yes, exactly," approved Simon. He grew more confident and became relaxed. The attorney was not only a good legal expert, but he was familiar with psychology too. He sounded like a friend, not the prosecution's representative. He must have realized Simon would accept sympathy in exchange for his words.

"This software makes seamless space for another one," Simon added, "which can go deeper and deeper, and we can go into servers all around the Solar System, where nobody else could." He smiled proudly to the camera drones.

Peter could not decide what would be better: Simon's incessant whining or this new, unstoppable swagger.

"Then you reached the server of the New Large Hadron Collider operated by CERN, didn't you Mr. Barrens?"

"Exactly," nodded Simon collaboratively. The dreadlocks were missing from his bald head, so he even resembled a rodent. "I mean, it went to the NLHC's database first and copied the whole drive into an external file."

"This was the file that you needed to give to your connections. Do you know anything about them?"

Simon got worried again, his confidence drained away. He exchanged a glance with his lawyer.

"We don't know anything about them, only that they paid very well."

The attorney used his inquisitorial look again.

"Don't you think that you connections could be terrorists?"

"I have no idea who they are," said Peter quietly when they stopped in the underground garage of a big shopping mall. This big black car had picked them up thirty minutes ago and taken them to the meeting place. "Since when have you cared who's paying for the job?"

"I don't really care—normally. But we normally don't break into a collider's database and control system running on twenty-eight-teravolt capacity. So, yeah, I'm interested a bit more."

"Whoever it is, he's rich beyond the dreams of avarice. This little disc is enough to pay us a salary for ten years!" waved Peter with the datadisc in his hand.

Another similar black car stopped next to them. The driver stepped to the rear window, which was rolled down a bit. A hand appeared in the hole with a briefcase. In the next moment, the disc and the briefcase had been duly exchanged. There were other discs next to the money with new fragments of code, which—as they were later instructed—they had to inject again into the NLHC control system.

"I don't want to know what they really do," said Peter when they'd returned to the rat hole. He started to unpack and load the codes into the NLHC control server. "It can be anything, I don't care. It's worth the gold for me!"

"It could be *hijack software*; I've never seen coding language like that before," said Simon, rattling a marshmallow's package. "Man, we might be taking control over the biggest Hadron Collider in the world!"

"When exactly did this happen?" Mr. Ortega asked the Swiss man sitting on the witness stand. Professor Hans Gossens was CERN Chief Director at the time of the van der Bruck Incident.

"I think it was in eighty-seven, in 2187. I led CERN at that time."

"That was before or after the verification of Higgs bosons?"

"This was well after the bosons, around the time when we found the Vanderbilt-particles."

"Can you shortly explain what are these particles, and what kind of role do they play in our universe?"

"I'll try," said the professor, adjusting his old-fashioned glasses, then activated the holographic projector with a remote control. "The existence of the Higgs bosons was predicted by Peter Higgs, the famous theoretical physicist, at the second millennium, but we only found the indelible evidence in later 2013–14. As you can see in these drawings," at his words, a big flower-shaped, colourful picture appeared in the space above the courtroom, "we could detect the path of a possible particle, the Higgs boson, after the collision. We didn't understand before where the mass had disappeared. The mass had been taken by the Higgs boson, and those trails came from that particle."

"And what about the Vanderbilt particles, Professor?"

"Yes, I'm just getting to that," nodded the professor changing to another hologram. "The particle predicted by Tim Vanderbilt was the missing link to another force whose origins we didn't understand. These were the graviton particles. Without knowing about them, these floating camera drones or even the artificial gravity wouldn't exist."

"Professor, how did you notice that the control of NLHC was not in your hands anymore?"

"When we built the collider under the icy surface of Antarctica, it was the biggest man-made structure, with a diameter of 260 kilometres. Due to the long distance and the amount of energy used, we controlled it over a protected network from the CERN building. This protected network was hacked by the van der Bruck group later."

Yeah, call us a group, you monkey, there are only two of us! But I could have done it all by myself, thought Peter.

"We started to worry when the first collision on 32 teravolts happened. We wanted to have only on 25 teravolts, but the collider did not react to the performance control or the emergency stop. But when it finally reached the 32 teravolts, it stopped automatically. After we looked through the hardware and the software, we didn't find anything that could explain this major malfunction. We stopped the system for two months to check all data collected from the detectors before we started the work again."

"What was the consequence of this event?"

"Well, you could see it on every news channel the day after."

"Peter, you have to watch this! Switch to the news on Channel 4!"

Peter hated when Simon called him at home, when they weren't working. In truth, they hadn't worked for months, they just spent all their money and relaxed.

"OK, shut up and calm down," he said and got up. It was six thirty, on Saturday morning, no less. "I wanted to sleep more, why don't you do the same?"

"The scientists at CERN made a remarkable discovery today," said the reporter on the TV. He stood in front of the CERN building under the heavy rain in his thick jacket. "The data recorded in all detectors are much more different than any of the previously recorded patterns. As Katrin Woolberg, chief scientist, said: 'Modern physics has arrived at a major milestone again.' She didn't say anything more about it, but the whole story will be revealed in detail at the press conference at seven. We'll come back live from the event, stay with us!"

"We did it, surely, not them!" Simon screamed with his painfully sharp voice, and Peter had to hold the communicator far from his ear. "We set a milestone, screw you!"

"We didn't set anything up, you moron, we did what we were paid to do." Peter got completely fed up with the Rat's outburst. Moreover, he thought he was funny.

"That's simple," he added, "everybody's been paid for something."

"And what have you been paid for, Mr. Roodeben?" asked Peter's lawyer, Craig Bolton, pulling his eyebrows up. The corpulent man on the witness stand couldn't seem to relax in the cameras' crossfire.

"I'm paid for making risk analysis. We go through the results with my team, and we analyse if there was a major error in the previous experiment that can lead to stopping the unsafe activity."

"So, basically, you're responsible for the safety of the super-project, which, in some cases, can put all of humankind in danger?"

Roodeben was sweating profusely. He was questioned as a witness, but if the lawyers did their job well, he could soon be accused. He had to be careful about what he said.

"I wouldn't say that the fate of all humankind would depend on our job, because the NLHC itself cannot put the globe in danger."

"You said *itself*, but if someone changed the control software, then it is possible."

The man took off his glasses and wiped away the mess of sweat drops.

"I think that my team and I are not responsible for what happened in NLHC. The complex checking of all systems and equipment didn't find any major error that could have led to that overdrive. The masked commands loaded by the two defendants were not made on our coding language, so the virus-killer engines could not find them."

The lawyer heatedly pointed to the dock.

"So do you think, Mr. Roodeben that these men, and only these two men, are responsible for the current situation?"

Peter felt that his lawyer—a modest Englishman from the Mars New Home Colony—was changing his tactic and wanted to emphasize the possibility of the collective responsibility.

"I don't know, sir," said Roodeben bewildered. "What is certain now, looking back to the fact, is that the system let them in. It let a piece of software written in an unknown language make an interaction with the control system of a multibillion-dollar project. I think this is a basic architectural problem . . ."

"What kind of architectural problem do you mean? —Jane, *Mars and Science*." The holographic figure of the reporter rose in the middle of the press conference. The room booked for the event turned out to be too small. They hadn't counted on the holoports coming from the colonies, which occupied the same amount of space as a flesh-and-blood person.

"I can only say that we've found a hole in the architectural design," said Katrin Woolberg, the chief scientist of NLHC. She had aged a lot in the past months due to overwork and lack of sleep. "We are sure that this caused the NLHC's overdrive. The collider had been operated above its specified and safe levels and didn't react to the emergency stop command."

"What will the consequences of this error be in regard to the global safety of the Earth-Mother Colony? —Robert, *Moon Colony, News Centre*."

"According to our current knowledge, the Mother Colony—or even the Solar System—is not in danger. In the past two months, skilled security experts looked through our system and didn't find anything else apart from this architectural problem," said the chief scientist, raising her hand to stop the incoming wave of questions. "Let me pass your next question to my colleague, Brittany Johnson, who will tell the real reason we've called you here. Brittany, please!"

"Thank you, Katrin," said the woman, appearing in the holoport at the end of the table. She changed the hologram floating above the people from the press.

"We've recorded this picture in the biggest detector of the NLHC. You can see that this sample doesn't show the same pattern as any normal collision we've experienced before. The trajectories of the particles are expressly structured. The trajectory patterns shows unique layout."

She changed the picture again.

"We concluded here after several weeks of work because we had to separate the trajectories from each other." The hologram turning in the middle of the room started to show a complex sign consisting of points. When the sign emerged from the series of points, the room was filled with surprised murmuring.

"Yes, this is what it looks like. Four letters, the M, the O, the R , and the E—these letter give the word MORE."

"MORE? What do you mean? Did the pattern resemble the English word *more*?" Simon's lawyer, Paul Vernon from the Moon Colony, asked Katrin Woolberg.

"Yes, it definitely shows that word," Katrin didn't understand what the lawyer was getting at.

"Mrs. Woolberg, how do you think it was possible to find this very common English word in one of the NLHC's detector created merely from quarks, leptons, and other subatomic particles?"

"It could be a message. An artificial intelligence might want to communicate with us this way. I know it's an absurd idea, but this was the best I could come up with. We excluded all possible errors, checked all systems, and we had to conclude that the message was real."

"What was your decision about the future experiments?"

"We agreed that we need to continue. We couldn't stop at the threshold of a scientific achievement that might be the biggest of the century or even in the history of humankind . . ."

Vernon stopped suddenly and turned to the hologram hovering above them.

"This is an invitation, Mrs. Woolberg. It says MORE, I want more and more experiments. Didn't you have serious misgivings about this?"

Peter was watching the news indifferently. After many months, they had to swing into action; they had uploaded a new intruder at the request of the secret employer.

He knew that it was all the worm's doing—this small piece of software was conducting the whole cacophonic orchestra—but he didn't care. He enjoyed the disharmony caused by this string of codes with all its advantages. One of these was, of course, the incredible amount of money he got for the worm's injection. That's how he'd been able to buy a luxury yacht—where he was drinking his ice-cold cocktail while his boat was stranded by a tropical storm on the coast of Malibu.

"The NLHC announced today that the recent experiment ended in a complete failure. At the first part of the experiment, the collider was working as expected, then it unexpectedly doubled its performance. It didn't respond to the emergency stop command as had happened six months ago. This led to the bizarre result that the collider is still operating at this very moment. Nobody is driving the proton beams, which are running at top speed. They tried to collide them with a concrete safety wall, but the beams didn't react to the electromagnets' polarization change. If the two beams were to collide at this speed, the resulting energy could be 38 tera-electron-volts. I would like to ask our expert about the consequences of such a collision; some even fear that it could lead to the total annihilation of the Earth. What do you think?"

"I don't think it could happen, we are completely safe," said the expert-looking man holding papers in his hand. "It's possible that the structure of space will change when this amount of energy is liberated. But this will only be in the smallest measure possible, which cannot be harmful for us. Although micro black holes can come into existence, but they would disappear right after their birth."

"What can you tell us about the micro black holes?"

"I can't say anything," said Peter staring at the attorney's eyes. He decided that he would stand his ground, and it worked this time.

"You want me to believe that when the worm injected by you took control over the biggest collider in the world and drove two proton beams—consisting of billions of particles—into each other, creating more than two thousand micro black holes, that you had no idea what a micro black hole was?"

"Exactly," said Peter throwing his hands up in mock despair. "Why would I care? I'm good at coding, but it doesn't mean I have to be interested in science."

Peter knew very well what micro black holes were, he had read well enough about them recently. These tiny creatures were small in size but enormous in gravity, and they could even alter the structure of space if they were born at the same time. They would swallow everything around them, of course, only at the subatomic level. Theoretically they didn't live long . . .

"Their lifecycles are short," said the attorney, as if he were finishing Peter's thought, "but we know that this assertion is incorrect in the case of numerous micro-sized black holes."

As you say, Big Man, thought Peter, *as you say. I don't care what you say, even if you repeat it a thousand times. But you can't make us the only scapegoat . . .*

"In such cases it can happen that the micro-sized black holes swallow each other and evolve to a bigger-than-atomic-sized black hole, which can eat more material from neighbouring space, isn't that right, Mr. van der Bruck?"

"Say whatever you want," Peter shook his head. "I have no clue about physics and the subatomic heck of which you speak."

The attorney suddenly grabbed the bar of the accused's desk and shouted at Peter, "Are you saying that these micro-sized black holes didn't form something bigger?"

"No, not at all," said the red haired man wearing a thick fur coat. He was in the NLHC's bunker, in the control room of the building-sized detector below the ice of Antarctica. "Although we counted more than 2,800. The concentration of the graviton particles proved that the black holes actually formed, but didn't unite to a bigger, massive black hole, which was rather surprising. But we have something here that is much more troublesome. You have to look at this."

The board had come from Geneva—all the big shots thronged into the control room, similarly covered in furs. They looked like mourning ladies next to a grave as they gathered around, as if they were in deep sorrow about the appearance of the blinking red dots in the middle of the screen.

"According to the data from the detector, this is an unstable point. Constant data flow coming from this uncertain structure of space."

"So, has something other than a black hole formed here?" asked Brittany Johnson, the project leader. There was real anxiety in her eyes.

"I wouldn't call it a black hole, rather a tear in the structure of space. Through this we are continuously receiving subatomic particles from somewhere beyond our dimension. We don't need to operate the collider to supply energy to this system; it became totally independent and self-sustainable."

The group stood in total shock in front of the fluorescent points. There were no words, all of them were trying to digest the explanation.

"I want to show you something else," said the scientist and changed the view on the screen to a more recognizable stream of signs. "The data has been flowing continuously from the moment the tear occurred. These strings were formed by those particles and connected to a totally harmless piece of software in the control program. The amount of data became bigger and bigger here."

A mixture of fear and admiration ran through the gathering. Some took off their coats as the situation got more heated.

"This little, inoffensive software was replaced a few months ago, but we didn't notice it. This is maintenance software that was updated regularly without any problem. Somebody took this out and put it back seamlessly here at the Mother Colony."

The murmurs changed to loud protests: "I don't believe it!" and "How could this happen?" repeated throughout the room.

"I think we have to report to the United Colony Council that the New Large Hadron Collider has been hijacked."

Mr. Ortega knew that he had to lift the sword, the *descabello*, because it was time to kill the broken bull fallen on its knees with a last, honoured stab. But there was nothing noble in this move, because his enemy was not a bull, but a whining rodent. Simon was already broken under the charges.

"Judge Kristensen, we didn't hijack it! We had no idea what we were doing!" shrieked Simon toward the bench. *Of course, when they were still free, Simon had boasted proudly to his friends that, "I'm controlling the world's most expensive machine,"* thought Peter. He would blow this whole case up and break it into pieces. There would be no safety responsibility, no collective responsibility, no architectural failure; the blame would be put completely on them.

All the work of the two lawyers would be finished in minutes in the frightened writhing of the Rat.

"Don't try to convince me. Tell me what you know, and I'll draw my own conclusion about it," said Judge Kristensen.

"We received the packages each month," said Simon, struggling with the words. "We had to inject them into the *nest*, which is a modified program..."

"You moron," Peter pushed the words through his teeth. All the cameras surged toward him to capture the moment when the carefully built defence plan would shatter into pieces.

"From whom did you get these packages?" attacked the attorney, with a pleased gesture. Obviously he felt he'd made good progress.

"I have no idea, I've never seen anybody. We just got the money and asked no questions. We injected the last package into the *nest*, and we never saw them afterwards. They've never called us again."

"Mr. Barrens, you've never cared about how dangerous it could be if this collider working with enormous power fell into the wrong hands? You've never thought that you committed a serious crime playing with the lives of so many billions of people?!"

Simon broke into tears, then exclaimed, "I thought about it, of course I thought, it was always in my mind, but he..." he stood up and pointed at Peter, "... but he always wanted to continue! He pulled me into this!"

"You lying, rotten rat!" shouted Peter standing up again, but he was subdued by the electric shock on his neck, wrists, and ankles. He dropped to the floor like a puppet. The guards placed him back in his seat, where he was lying paralysed, eyes blurred, and dripping saliva for the rest of the time. With the last sparkle of his mind, he realized they'd lost, it was finished. Then he lost consciousness.

"So, Mr. Barrens, let me summarise the last sentences of the verdict based on your statement," said Ortega, shining. He held Simon with an iron grip to wring him out and throw him away like a squeezed lemon.

"Mr. van der Bruck and you were hired by an unknown person, or persons, to break into the world largest collider's control software and hijack it. You said you didn't know the purpose of this intrusion, but you did everything as agreed and got your payment as return service. Is that true, Mr. Barrens?"

"Yes, it is."

"When data started to flow through the tear in space—formed from the micro-sized black holes—to a piece of software implanted by you, and wrote in an unknown language, you fled from Earth, is that right?"

"Yes, it is." Simon's voice shattered into tears.

"Although, if you had given yourself up, you could have helped to stop the process, is that right?"

"The software was coded in some kind of unknown language, as if it were alien to Earth . . ." protested Simon. "We couldn't do anything!"

"And then, when this unknown piece of software restarted the collider and made particle collisions bigger than ever, then you could still have given yourself up, couldn't you, Mr. Barrens?"

"Yes, I could've, but it would have been too late!"

The attorney slowly walked away, hinting that he thought he had finished the case.

"Thank you, Judge Kristensen. The prosecution has finished procedure. I hand over the case to you to deliver a verdict."

Milder judgment was pronounced for Simon. The extenuating circumstances were that he couldn't assess the weight of his act, he was cooperative and he showed signs of remorse.

Remorse, my ass! Poor little Rat. He could suffer in one of the prisons of Europa for the crime he committed against humankind.

His long hair was floating around him in the weightless interior of the cabin like seaweed—or like elephant grass in the storm, as he'd seen ages ago on an ancient documentary. Strange, that he was thinking about that . . . right now. He could not move his hands, they were handcuffed to the sides of the rounded window. They wanted him to see all along, minute by minute. This was part of his punishment. As he was falling into the void . . . into the continent-sized, omnivorous glowing white hole. This was the new term for the tear in space structure.

It had a proper name too: the van der Bruck hole. The first ever white hole had been named after him.

He couldn't publish a book after all, but this mysterious thing would stay forever. And would become larger. There was nobody on the Mother Colony anymore. Mars, and Europa had reached their limit, couldn't keep up with the ever-growing number of refugees. The Moon would be in danger soon, although its orbit was outside of the white hole's event horizon.

He didn't know why, but his mother's face appeared frozen in front of him. It stood there for a countless moment after starting to fade away.

And everything became spaghetti-long as in the black hole. Even his thoughts transformed to a spaghetti-thought about the code written in the unknown language. Perhaps when he reached the other side he would be able to decode it.

Then he would work for them, those, on the other side. It wouldn't matter who they were. It could be anybody who paid a lot, and this was what mattered, wasn't it?

IX.

Soul Trap

The chief medical director was watching the busy boy through the tinted window of his office; the boy was thinner than he expected. He'd really thought that a lively man would come to relieve the pain of the patients in the final stage. But not a young twenty-something...

"You promised a *colleague*," said the chief medical director, strongly emphasizing the last word, "who has wide knowledge and long years of experience in hospice service." He stopped speaking, looking apprehensively at the man standing at his side; the man just shook his head and smiled.

"You have to believe me, he's not the fragile boy he looks at first sight."

"No? Then who is he?"

"I can't tell you that, his real personality is protected. His name is George now. You have to accept my word that he's really the best in this field. He's been through a lot and is very experienced," said the man, the regional director of the prominent clone company The Young Body for the Future. The chief medical director kept watching the boy as he carried on with his job in a professional manner. All the patients loved him from the moment he'd entered the room this morning; he obviously brought happiness into their tormented lives. They kept questioning him, continually asking for favors and help, and he fulfilled one request after another.

"Indeed . . ." said the chief, struggling to accept the truth that this scrawny kid was really good. He was bloody good. Even better than himself, the chief doctor, although they couldn't have more than fifty years of work experience between them.

He went around the table to show his guest to a seat. The regional director, once seated before him, took a folder out of his briefcase.

"I'm very happy that you've accepted our offer, sir. The Young Body for the Future has more than one-and-a-half million clone bodies rented and two hundred thousand available bodies for new clients. Our newest project—in which your institute can participate—is the Soul Donation."

The doctor lifted his eyebrows and looked to his negotiation partner, intrigued.

"I know it sounds strange," the man in the black suit continued, "but it's really true; we're not looking for organ donors, but soul donors in this project."

"Maybe I misread your preliminary brochures, but I didn't see anything like that in there. You offered us a colleague with hospice experience."

"You're right. But we made the offer in exchange for participating in our research and development project."

The chief medical director became concerned—he picked up the documents from the table and quickly went through them again.

"Yes, I see now, but I thought the *expert*—heavily emphasizing the word and pointing to the boy—would do statistics, surveys, and the like..."

"He'll do those kinds of tasks too, of course. But his main objective now is to recruit colleagues, like himself. Namely, we've implanted the first donated soul into this young clone body."

"Oh—" said the doctor with wide eyes. It seemed that his opinion had suddenly changed about the boy on the other side of the window. He seemed to be a tireless soul in a tireless body.

"I see I've captured your attention," said the clone expert and opened the holographic folder in front of him. There was an impressive, three-dimensional display of action above the table with soldiers in battle, pilots flying with jets on parabolic courses, men embarking from military freighters and jumping off tanks.

"The army is our biggest customer. Not enough people want to be a soldier nowadays, so they need well-trained clones with strong personalities who can fight for peace. Our peace."

"Our patients are already standing beside their graves. I don't think they would like to fight. Many of them have given up already."

"Of course, I know," the regional director gave an obligatory smile. He was disturbed by the incomprehension that was interrupting his usual sales pitch. He had done this very effectively many times before, as an experienced clone salesman, which had catapulted him into the chair of the highest regional position.

"We won't use them on the frontline. They'd go to hospitals, as George came to your institute."

It sounds logical, thought the doctor. These terminally ill people would be able to more emphatically help the suffering soldiers coming from the battles, and they would be able to deal with the problems more efficiently.

"These terminally ill people would be able to more emphatically help the soldiers..."

"... and they would be able to deal with the problems more efficiently," interrupted the chief medical director. "I've just had the same thought."

"Brilliant," said the clone expert with a victorious smile. "Then we almost share a common view in this matter."

Not just almost, speculated the doctor and looked at the boy again. There was some kind of marvelous balance and organization in his movement, like in a heavenly symphony. *This boy is awesome!*

"It's clear that this partnership will be fruitful for you," he said, looking back to the clone salesman, "but what is the advantage for us?" As he finished the sentence, there was already another hologram in front of him.

"Here's the new wing of your institute—The Shelter of Souls. The institutes participating in our program receive this newly built extension from us. The staff members will be clones with donated souls. Specialized, highly experienced clones who know life and death inside-out."

"Like him . . ." said the chief medical director, watching the patients and his new colleague again. The boy was so gentle, devoted as he himself had never been in his thirty years of care. *He's damn good!* Almost as if he weren't human . . .

"Exactly like him," agreed the dark-suited man. A hopeful smile arose at the side of his lips—he knew that the negotiation was close to the end, and it would be finished with the most favorable conclusion.

"All right," nodded the doctor, "I accept your offer, and I'll give the boy a three-month probation period; he might live up to our expectations." He still felt offended by the young man's obvious skills.

"We have a deal," the clone salesman reacted quickly with a bright, white smile. "Just sign here."

After dealing with the official papers, the chief medical director was still watching his newly hired staff member through the tinted window. He did not care anymore about his age or the fact that he was too thin and weak for the job. There was something in him that he could not deny or resist. Something unearthly. Something angelic.

"And how will he harvest those souls?" he asked, finally turning to the clone salesman, who seemed to have gained back his confidence and must've felt himself very rich.

"With this little trap," the man lifted the small box in his hand. "He has the ability to guide the souls to this box instead of letting them leave the world."

"I hope so . . ." nodded the chief medical director, already focusing further, behind the boy, to the place where the Dignity Hospice Center's new wing, The Shelter of Souls, would soon emerge. A wonderful, prosperous future to come!

Oh this boy; he is unbelievably good!

*

When Lorance was named Linda . . .

"My name is George."

He felt no resentment toward the relatives, although they had crossed the line between vulgarity and politeness.

"Look, we don't care who you are or what you think about our decision," said the man, jabbing a finger into the male nurse's chest to emphasize his words. "My wife and I decided to give our permission for *soul donation*. After signing the contract, they said the staff would be helpful and cooperative. And who is here to make trouble? A twenty-something kid, who's giving a lecture about morality instead of doing his job!"

George looked at the girl in the bed. She'd been lying there for two years since her car accident—she was brain-dead. The doctors said she could maintain only her vegetative functions, although George knew that wasn't true. She had been out of her body several times—floating between the ceiling and the bed—when the doctors had tried to reanimate her. Although she'd begged the staff not to repeat the resuscitation again, because life had no meaning in her body anymore, they could not hear her. At the request of the family, they kept her alive, and each time she had to go back to her damaged body. George saw her struggling back to the broken corpse through her head. It was not a heartwarming sight and reminded George of the unpleasant event he'd been through when his name was Georgij.

"I'm only saying that your relative's will can be totally different from the option that you have chosen."

The patient's sister attacked him furiously, "Where did you get this idea? Are you communicating with the dead? Why do they use mediums in hospice centers?"

"I'm not a medium. I'm a specialist in human souls. Believe me; your sister isn't dead. Her body is broken, but her soul is healthy."

"I've had enough!" said the man, throwing the official papers onto the bed. "It is written here in black and white; we're offering my sister-in-law's soul for donation. No further discussion!" He finished and turned to his wife, "Honey, tell somebody competent here to switch off Linda's machines. You," he looked at George, full of hatred, "you should mind your own business!"

"Wouldn't you like to bring your sister back to life at all costs? Even in another body?" said the woman giving George a reproachful look and stormed out to the corridor.

The place suddenly filled with doctors and nurses who set Linda's body free from tubes and syringes. They switched all life support systems off while the scanners moved back and the monitors blanked.

George placed the small box next to Linda's face. He had learned the process in the center of The Young Body for the Future cloning company in the past two months. He flipped off the safety cover with ease, while the lid divided into two equal parts. Blue light emerged from the gap. George took Linda's lock of hair and inserted it. He pulled down the blanket from the young woman, placing it at the end of the bed.

The small screen on the side of the box filled with details; the DNA's double helix appeared on it. It recorded all the data of Linda's body in fifteen seconds. Then an azure halo surrounded the corpse—small laser-like beams scanned the form for thirty seconds before retracting back inside the box.

One of the doctors looked at George. "You can take the body now," he nodded. She was taken on a floating bed. Linda's sister broke into tears as she saw Linda's remains moving away from her.

"And now—" she asked hopelessly, "what will happen now?"

"Don't cry. Everything is alright now."

George knew that Linda's soul was around there somewhere, but he also knew he could not waste time explaining.

"I'll activate the *memory-body* now. This is the life-like representation of your sister's body that we've recreated from Linda's memories from the time before the accident."

"But there's nothing there," said the man, flabbergasted.

"I'm here! Look up! Everything is alright!"
When she spoke to her sister, she noticed her own, unharmed body on the bed. She became confused for a moment. She floated

up through the ceiling, up to a higher level, then back; the body was still there. A wonderful, unbroken corpse; that was why she did not understand her sister's sorrow. It looked like everything was alright with this body, although she remembered the horrifying noise of the accident and the chaos that followed it. But this body looked healthy and recovered. It was painful to squeeze herself back into the broken one, but it might be different with this new one.

"It's impossible," the woman shook her head, her eyes flew back and forth between the bed and George. She was looking for something tangible, a flesh-and-blood person that she recognized. But there was nothing like that in the room apart from themselves.
"I ask you to stay silent now . . ." said George gently.
Linda's soul was hovering an arm's length from him; he could see it. Her soul-body was glowing in the dark as well as the memory-body created by the soul trap. The young woman did not understand the situation and was constantly asking questions. He tried to answer all of them. But something went wrong because Linda's soul left the room, straight through the wall into the corridor. The relatives could not sense anything from these events.

"This cannot be my body," thought Linda. She flew through the corridor and stopped above the floating bed with a covered body. She could not look below the sheet, but she recognized the form. But she didn't feel comfortable anymore with the old body. She followed it for a short time and then she turned back. She had to leave this world. A black, swirling hole opened in the ceiling; she could see the bright, warm light at the end.
She knew the light already. Unbelievably strong love radiated from it, infusing her soul-body.
The light spoke to her.

Then she saw her past as a movie. The light, this loving entity, highlighted some events from the series of pictures. The best and the worst. It did not want to shame her, and it loved her even more when those disgraceful, uncomfortable pictures arrived.

She had been a prostitute. The long period of rough times could have made her sad, but she felt reassuring comfort instead.

Then the light faded away. Linda wanted to follow, but it made clear to her that she had to stay behind.

She descended through the ceiling, back to the room where her relatives were standing next to that stranger, who was a bit familiar too. He could communicate with her like the loving light. She stood hovering in front of his face.

"This is not my real body," she said. "What do you want from me?"

"I want you to trust me. You will not be harmed. I am George," spoke the boy without moving his lips.

"I'm Linda. If I don't occupy this body, my time will finish in this world. It's so strange that time exists here."

"Don't worry. God cannot be evaded. He knows about everything," said the boy. "He doesn't let anything happen without reason."

Linda's memory-body started to oscillate and then faded away—this was only visible to George, the relatives couldn't see anything with their earthly eyes. The lid of the box slid back to the original position and Linda's face appeared on it.

"Is there a problem?" asked the man, puzzled. The last five minutes had been uneventful for them.

"Not at all," George said, smiling and reaching to shake his hand. "We thank you for your generous donation. The Young Body for the Future Consortium will transfer the agreed payment to your account as soon as possible."

**

When Bernard was named Bill . . .

Lorance felt that it would be hard with Bill. He was not an easy man.

"Suck it! You all can suck it, everybody in this damned institute!" said the rude, old man and spat on the floor. The spittle made a disgusting red patch on the floor.

"That's what I gave you that little tray for," said Lorance and carefully cleared the paved floor.

"I don't care. I gave orders all of my life and others obeyed me. That's not going to change now at the end of my life; you'll do what I want, too," he said with a delirious reflection in his eyes.

"I've paid for this. I bought your service too," he continued with a rattle in his throat. The rattling turned to choking and finished with a coughing attack.

"He . . . he . . . help me!" he said, gesticulating vehemently in the middle of the attack. Lorance did not move. She found it difficult to do nothing, but she wanted to break the man.

"For God's sake!" he begged.

Lorance mixed oxygen with evaporated painkiller and put the mask on Bill's face. There was clear hatred in his blurry eyes even through the pain and struggle. When he was better, he threw the mask away.

"Why are you angry, Bill?"

The man didn't answer, he exhaled and huffed deeply. He needed some time to gather himself again.

"Because I love my body, and I hate that I need to buy a new one. I want to live in my own body, but the doctors aren't capable of making it work. I bought three lungs, two livers, and I could buy all the other organs from the list that you can make . . . but something doesn't work."

"Despite the organ technology's success, your body is growing older and older," said Lorance regretfully. "It isn't able to keep up with a new heart or liver."

"What do you know about aging?"

Lorence had no experience with natural aging in her new clone body. But in her pale memories—where her name was still Linda—she lived and worked on the street where her body had become drawn-out and worn. She felt aged a hundred years after one cold day outside.

"Have you ever thought about the priceless spiritual values?" she asked smiling to Bill. Lorance sat on the bedside in spite of the man's disapproving look.

"Don't fool me! There is no priceless value anymore, the soul can be donated! I've just signed a contract to sell mine for scientific purposes. You can buy anything with your money nowadays . . ." he spat out every word while retreating back to the far side of the bed.

Lorance was happy to hear the news. She couldn't imagine that Bill would be the third to join the team. There was so much rudeness and aggression in him that even flooded Lorance's patience sometimes. When it happened, she had to wait until he calmed down a bit.

After a few minutes, she suddenly grabbed his hand. Bill's eyes rounded, pure shock was reflected back from the bottom of the well-deep pupils. He fought for some seconds, trying to pull his hands away, but then gave up. With his eyelids closed tight and his mouth squeezed haughtily, he bore Lorance's caress.

"You don't need to do this," he hissed. He looked like a snake caught by his tail and struggling to escape from his tormentor, ready to turn back at any moment to bite into the hand. But Bill was sick, awfully sick. He could not bite anymore. Lorance knew this.

"We humans do so many things we shouldn't," she answered. "This is the unique nature of our race; sometimes we do irrational and useless things to make someone happy."

Lorance felt Bill's hand finally relax. This was the first breakthrough since they had appointed her as his nurse. When the construction of the new wing had finished, Bill became her first patient in the Dignity Hospice Center.

George was still her mentor, as he had been from the beginning. She knew him from the time when she was called Linda. He was the only one who had been able to communicate with her, and she appreciated this. Most of her past memories faded away, only one stayed with her: the loving light.

Lorance was drawn back to the present by the beeping noise of the heart monitor, although her unconscious soul had already sensed that Bill was ready to leave the physical world.

She left one last caress on his wrinkled, worn palm and turned off the life-support machines. She did as she was instructed; Bill had no money to pay for further service, so it had to be ended. The only reason he had been kept alive was that he'd signed the contract for soul donation. According to the deal, he could stay two months longer in the institute.

"A soul worth only two months extra time," she heard from the depths of her own soul.

After the second month, after a long fight, this was a great achievement in their relationship. She could meet with Bill's broken soul that could now have a new perspective and purpose in life.

She prepared the trap and placed it to Bill's temple. The box started the scanning process when Bill appeared above his head.

His new radiant, bright white soul-body did not remind her of the gray-faced corpse that was now covered with a sheet.

Bill had no relatives, friends, or anybody to bid him farewell from his bedside. It was only Lorance, who had kept fighting and arguing with him for the past two months.

And God, who let him back to the *memory-body* prepared by the soul trap.

Lorance could not stop smiling while she closed the lid of the box. It was so good to see God's plan at work.

***

The regional director of The Young Body for the Future Clone Consortium was walking the floor in the chief medical director's office. The soles of his shiny shoes tapped out the silent seconds with each step. They counted sixty mute seconds when he finally stopped and looked Bernard in the eye.

"Bernard, please . . ." he asked in a bland tone, although he was normally ruder with clones. "You've been here in the Center for four months already, and you could not save one single soul. Why?"

Bernard smiled gently to the clone salesman and the doctor who was sitting behind his desk.

"I've followed all instructions and protocols, sir," he said politely. There was nothing to indicate the rude, churlish style he'd had when his name was Bill. His soul had become embellished in the loving light.

"I don't understand," said the doctor, shaking his head. He suddenly stood up and walked to Bernard's chair—rising dominantly above him, as if to say by his body language, "You're in trouble."

"Everything went smoothly with the first two clones, then he came, and all of them stopped working. We have to dissolve all contracts and pay the damages" said the chief medical director, turning to the clone salesman.

"Please calm down, sir," the clone salesman stopped him. "I'll deal with him," he said, waving to Bernard. Both went to the side of the room, where the dark-suited man whispered in Bernard's ear. "You can't leave me in this deep shit," he said while his eyes were running back and forth between the doctor's white-coated figure and his clone. "My position, or maybe my whole career, is at stake." He was nervous; his forehead was wet with sweat.

"I'm deeply sorry, sir," said Bernard respectfully. "We did everything as before. There was no change in the protocol. But the rest won't fail because of us. The souls can decide whether they leave or stay, but the higher power, or entity—as you call it—has a say in the matter."

"Don't talk my head off with this higher-power stuff," grimaced the clone salesman. "It's only an advertisement to get more clients. Anyway, faith is in crisis all around the world. There is no higher entity. If it actually did exist, we wouldn't have sold so many clone-bodies in the past decades."

"The clone-renters don't die," said Bernard. "They're still alive at the moment their souls are implanted into the new body. Our clients turn to us when they're already dead. The two situations are completely different."

The dark-suited man stroked his chin and looked straight into Bernard's eyes. "What you're doing is sabotage. I could easily annihilate all of you."

Bernard didn't look scared. He remained unruffled. "According to paragraph 20.042 of the United Colony Law, we are considered *reborn-clones*. We have our own individual souls, we are not renters, and we have no body in a stasis-cabin, which means we're citizens of the Solar System with full power. If you annihilated us, it would be considered a criminal act. If we were to get hurt or die, our lawyer would contact the papers. The media would be more than helpful to report about the disappearance of the first three reborn-clones."

The dark-suited man kept a stiff upper lip. He slowly placed his hand to Bernard's shoulder and squeezed it.

"You need to know which side you're playing on," he hissed and turned to the chief medical director.

"It's alright," he raised his hands toward the impatient doctor, "we had to talk about some important points. They need some time, that's all they want. I suggest we meet again in three months."

In three months we can save lot of souls, thought Bernard, when he joined his friends in the corridor. Lorance and George were already waiting for him. They understood each other without words. After a welcoming smile, they left toward the cafeteria.

"Look at them," said an envious nurse at the desk, "I always wanted to have friends like them."

"Oh, me too. They're marvelous, although some people have doubts about them," the woman next to the nurse agreed with her colleague. "Since they are still clones, aren't they?"

"Yes, they are, but with an incredible irradiation! Did you hear them preaching in the cafe last week? So charismatic!"

"Especially George. He's a really talented speaker, as if he's been doing this all his life. I heard from one of our patient's daughters that he talked to her mother about God. He talked about Heaven, the afterlife, and that she shouldn't worry; she'll have a new, perfect body on the other side. After he finished, the old woman was so peaceful and she just slept. She hasn't woken up since."

"I think this is the reason for the donation program's failure."

"Definitely. Who would want to come back to this world after spending their whole life in a broken body—if somebody reassured them that life on the other side is so wonderful?"

"I wouldn't," laughed the nurse.

"Shh... they're coming."

The two women fell silent when the chief medical director accompanied the clone salesman to the exit. The emotions of their disturbed souls could be seen on their faces, radiating their worries into the physical world.

"George could help them too," whispered one nurse to the other, and they turned back to their daily work.

✳✳✳✳

At the beginning, when George was named Georgij...

"Medic! Where's the damn medic?"

The sand of the South Australian beach drank the blood quickly, instead of letting it run in a red rill, then a bigger creek. The red stream had found its way through Kiran's fingers when he pushed down on the wounds between Georgij's ribs. The bleeding man, a Marine, had come from the Independent Russian Republic and embarked with the first wave in the middle of the battle against New-China, fighting with energy beams. Kiran's Indian Unit arrived as the rear-guard in the second wave with hovercrafts. The Russians almost reached the line of the mobile shields—the floating drones that made wide protective arcs from charged energy fields—when the volley of fire broke through on the side.

"Medic, for God's sake!" shouted Kiran helplessly. He knew that Georgij's biochip had already sent the alarm, but he had to pour all of his rage into this shout. He knew Georgij closely;

he was the United Colony Disembarkation Regiment's young chaplain. He had a noble and bright soul, although there was no place for faith in Kiran's life. Through the years he'd spent in battles with Georgij, he'd become convinced that Georgij was a man of God.

"Crovavaya Voyna (*bloody war*)," he heard from the firing line before Cheslav skidded next to them. He was close enough to Kiran that the language module of his biochip could translate the Russian to English.

"They promised three shield drones, but we only got one," said Cheslav, breathing heavily and pointing to the drone floating a short distance from them. "They say the army used all the rest up north, where the wealthiest and bloodiest of the Asian conflicts are ongoing. And here we're undefended from the side!"

He crept next to the wounded man and placed a half-palm sized scanner over Georgij's chest. The teardrop-shaped floating medical equipment started its analysis. Cheslav took some sealant powder to close the wound and waved to Kiran to lift his hand. The blood sprayed all over the place.

"This is not good. Definitely not good," said Cheslav when the scanner stopped over the heart and signaled an alarm. "The shot blew up the ribs, and the bone fractions cut the heart's chambers into pieces! He might have thirty seconds left . . ."

"Call the copter!" Kiran bawled at the medic. "There are enough cloned hearts on the aircraft carrier . . ."

"They can't land here! Even with full shield they wouldn't survive more than a minute," said Cheslav, looking straight into the Indian's eye. "I'll prepare the trap."

Kiran held the wound again, but there was no sense in it anymore; Georgij died without another word.

Kiran had just realized what the medic said. "No! Let him leave!"

Cheslav disregarded him and placed the little box next to Georgij's temple. He entered the soldier's ID number and activated the trap.

"I said let him leave!" Kiran was serious now, he pushed his energy weapon to Cheslav's head.

"Yes, Kiran, I would love to, but they will take us to the military court. The Young Body for the Future Consortium is the army's biggest supplier. This is the reason we have such strict orders to use the trap!"

Kiran put the weapon down, his face distorted with rage.

"Georgij was a man of God, and if God exists, he won't let him back to this world. His soul will not let itself be tricked or confused by the trap," he said finally with resignation.

Cheslav covered the dead *physical body* of the chaplain; meanwhile, the box started flickering and drew Georgij's unbroken *memory-body* into the space. Energy blasts ripped apart the nearby vehicles, engines rumbled, and explosions swallowed the soldiers' tormented cries. Both looked up as if Georgij's soul were up there, thinking about returning. But they both hoped deeply that their friend was already on the way to the other side.

Georgij saw his two friends. He saw them down there with his body, approximately half a meter away. He shouted to them, but they didn't hear him. He wanted to touch them with the shining soul-body, but his hand only went through their bodies.

Then he suddenly heard the voice, "Go back, you still have things to do in this world."

He saw a remarkably unbroken body lying on the sand. It was not as damaged as he had expected. It looked young and powerful, as it had at the beginning of his service, when he entered the army. He looked into his friends' eyes one last time; he hoped they saw him.

"Don't argue, everything is alright. I have to stay with you. I have to save some souls. Do you hear me?"

Thereafter, he felt a strong push and woke up in a young clone-body.

And he knew perfectly what he had to do.

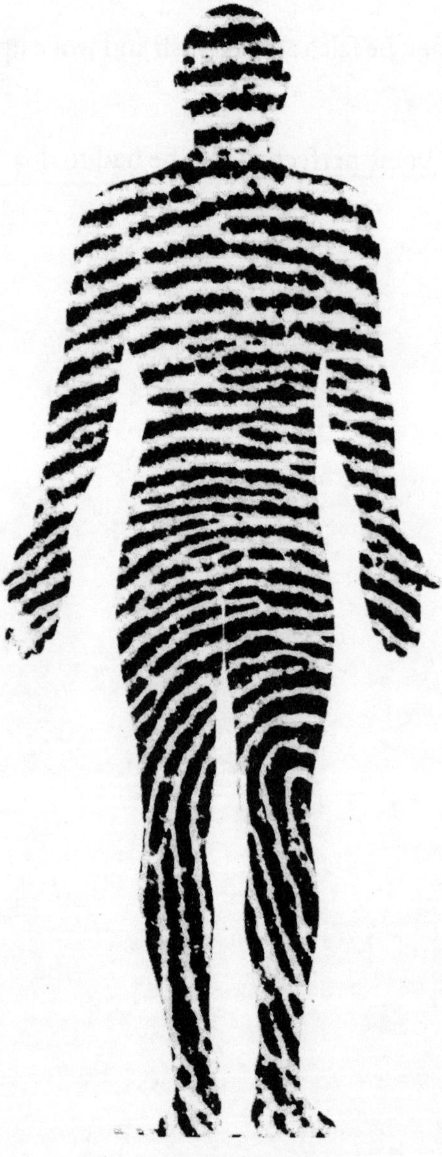

X.

The Identity

Joaquin hesitated in the half-open doorway, hand on the doorknob, and turned to look back into the dirty motel room. The wallpaper was peeling, a greasy stain marked the spot where other guests had rested their heads to watch TV from the bed. Struggling to hold the old tube TV was a battered console, the crossbars of its doors and drawers broken and hanging askew. There was a fist-sized hole in the built-in cupboard, with graffiti beside it—*Suck it!* The bedclothes, covered in dark red patches, lay on the floor. He hadn't used them; they obviously weren't clean enough. There was no detergent in existence strong enough to clean the grime ingrained here in the underworld. Well below New Cloud York.

But he changed his mind, and went back into the room. He went to stand before the faded mirror hanging behind the TV set—its sheen still reflected the past, hidden under its shattered surface. It broke his face into triangles and trapezoids, completely changing its shape. He had tried to become acclimated to his young and unfamiliar features in the past months, but he was so suddenly and utterly adult. He'd had no childhood, no time for the intimate self-reflection of the normal human lifespan.

On the console's broken, shiny shelf, official papers were piling up in a tower. The top one was a postcard from the cadets of his class, obscene drawings beside the jokes and the names. Deployment locations, coordinates, the last memories of a graduating group. Maybe that was the last known, physical trace of all he had left behind.

The duffle bag was on the bed. It was a camouflaged, *one-hundred-fifteen-kilogram curse*. Further to the left lay the military draft, stuck beneath the dirty sheets.

A few minutes ago he had been resolved. When he'd received the first alarm on his biochip that warned him he would be late for the draft, he ignored the signal easily. But now, standing in front of the mirror watching his own scattered face . . . he hesitated.

He had a creased, dirty note—written with old graphite pencil—in his hand. There was a list with seven names on it, but he'd already struck out four. Could he find his identity hidden behind these names?
He kept only three names from the Big Disk, from up there, where all the wealthy and rich lived. He could find out more about the other four, but he didn't want to be violent. Although he could; he was good at that, he was trained to kill.

When he finally did leave the room, the door closed with a mechanical noise, echoing down the long corridor. It was four o'clock, dawn. He had to reach New Cloud York before the sun rose.

He had a special ID in case of mobilization, which gave him free entry everywhere. Even to the elite part of the Disk.

He got on the *Upway* speed-bus. The chairs were orphaned in the morning emptiness, there were only two uniformed officers at the back. Because of the constant, turbulent situation, it was a new regulation that they be stationed on all lines to strengthen the police and army presence. The stock market had collapsed, and all the smoking, rotten remains of the dying economy covered Manhattan's streets.

Joaquin sat in the front; he pulled his sports bag beside him and turned up his collar. Cold morning wind would rush in between the closing doors in a moment when the flying bus departed the cracked asphalt. The burning fire—fed by old furniture, on top of the barricade at the front—coloured the windshield blood-red. It was a miracle that they'd still kept this bus stop. Without it, he would have to go three blocks from here to the flooded tunnels.

Joaquin noticed a scarecrow hanging on the post of the stop; the ultimate symbol of the evil banker—fat with luxury, rich and rapacious. The wind playfully picked an ember from the fire and deposited it in the eye of the puppet.

And then the bus, the flying Greyhound, started its spiral flight up to the Disk, while the rich and wealthy scarecrow followed its path with burning eyes.

*

He had to get off at the outer ring; the bus coming from the down side wasn't going any further. From here he had to take a taxi or walk. But there was definitely no time for walking, only thirty minutes left until sunrise.

Sunrise was the key element in the life of Hugh Swen Kingdon; his name was the first on the list. He left home a few minutes before sunrise to jog to the private sports complex behind the luxury villas. Hugh was the leader of the biggest lobby group; he traded with huge political influence. It was a power that could easily transfer to money, and Hugh did this extremely well. He had become the leading figure of weapons lobby because he saw the advantages emerging with the impending war in Asia. The state of emergency was escalating as he'd expected and helped him to convey his political ideas to the public: "Self-defence for Every Citizen" was his slogan. Many centuries before, America had forfeited the right to own guns when the fifty-second amendment was repealed. But now they were back on the market, and arms trading had peaked again. A new law was introduced—*The Evolution of Guns*, as the people called it nowadays.

Joaquin overheard a debate about it, right there on the taxi radio. The speaker said that Hugh Swen Kingdon had changed a lot recently. Instead of being the leader of the gun lobby, as everyone had expected, he was retracting and had almost become the opposition.

The yellow floating cab landed gently on the pavement. Joaquin paid with his chip, ten new dollars to the driver as a tip. The army gave him enough to cover his expenses on his holidays, but he only spent half.

The Golden Greek Era Recreation Centre was situated in the middle of a well-kept grove of olive trees. It contained a golf club, a fitness centre, and several running tracks, all surveyed by armed guards. Due to the state of emergency, they'd probably increased the security level.

The officer looked at the small screen of the scanner after invoking data from Joaquin's biochip. He inspected the paper ID to validate it.

"Soldier," the officer saluted him, giving back the ID. "You only have a few hours left before debarkation."

"True," said Joaquin with a strained smile, "but I can have a little jog before I say goodbye."

"All right," nodded the guard, "and . . . take care out there."

Joaquin waved and ran up the marble stairs through the olive tree grove to the track. He sat down on one of the wooden benches and prepared his gear; he put on his running shoes and placed his boots beside him. He hung his raincoat on the back of the bench.

Then he meticulously limbered up his muscles. His young body was valuable, he had to take good care of it—they'd spent a lot of time and money to shape him perfectly at the intergovernmental organization where he was employed. The monotonous rhythm of movements, lifting his legs and arms, made him relaxed. His personal thoughts vanished and he became a soldier again.

Meanwhile, the sun finally arrived and made a bright crescent below the arch of the entrance. The dancing yellow glow indicated that the actor in the main role would soon be here. The shining star slowly climbed the granite-paved path and reached the geometrical focus point of the arch; it stopped there as if it would wait for Hugh. At least that was Joaquin's first impression.

It didn't have to wait there long; the man's silhouette slowly filled the enlarging fiery background. He ran with well-composed movements, circling his arms, giving all the muscle groups a full warm-up as he came up the hill. His athletic figure slowly overtook the poplar in the background as he came closer to Joaquin and energetically jumped up the four stairs separating the track from the rest area.

Joaquin was amazed.

Hugh looked surprised to see him, the only other devoted sportsman to wake up with the sun. He nodded politely then cut into the inner track.

Joaquin had to catch up because time was running even faster than Hugh, the first man from his list. He wanted to concentrate on the runner and not on the luxury environment he'd never seen before. The complex looked like an archaic stadium, with Ionic and Doric pillars in the middle—some of them already broken in half, with grass climbing around the base. Highly decorated wall-fountains produced fresh water in the middle of this earthly Eden, surrounded by ruined tympanums and arcades. This artificially made scene symbolized the existence and transience of the ancient Greek Civilization, here, above the clouds. *Like the heaven of Greek mythology, Mount Olympus,* thought Joaquin.

Hugh Swen Kingdon had already done a full circle, passing Joaquin. He didn't look over, he was already used to the young man's presence. They were alone but for the birds circling above them—the people on the Big Disk were just starting to wake up. Faded traffic noise rose from afar, polluting the archaic idyll of the two men.

Joaquin took up the rhythm with a few short jumps. He was running against the clock, but he didn't want to frighten the man ahead of him. He simply wanted to synchronize his tempo, to breathe and move together with him—to feel his sweat's bitter odour, to see the well-balanced movement of his hip and knee. He wanted to delve into him until he could dwell in the details, the minutiae of the self, which might give him the whole picture in the end.

Tiny rubber fragments hit Joaquin's shin when he reached the man. These hailed from Hugh's white running shoes, a titillating shower on Joaquin's leg with every stride. So he decided to come up on Hugh's side and perfectly catch up with him. He didn't want to wait any longer to meet the man.

Hugh apparently didn't take notice of him; he didn't alter his rhythm at all when Joaquin came up beside him. He thought Joaquin would pass him and only looked at his new companion after one quarter of a circle.
Then Hugh started to play with the speed, intentionally slowing; he wanted Joaquin to take the lead. Joaquin didn't want to be intrusive, so he increased his speed a bit, but stayed close to Hugh. He could see the man's rhythmically waving body above his left shoulder. Then he gradually slowed back down, so they ran side-by-side again.

The sun climbed slowly above the tympanums and shaded the long, straight lines of the red running track with a chilling, fresh shadow. The two human bodies seemingly became one unified machine; their shoes scattered the tiny rubber fragments in sync and they broke the shadow line at the same moment, jumping into the sun's photon-beams as one. There was some kind of ethereal devotion or unearthly humility in their synchronicity.

Joaquin knew he could not spend more time in this ideal and unforgettable state, as they had been for the last two laps. He had to move on, to the next person on the list. It was a pity, because Hugh Swen Kingdon surely felt something about their connection, about this unified dance in life. Seemingly, he did not want to slow down or overtake Joaquin anymore but stayed with him, round by round, with great devotion. But Joaquin wanted more—he wanted to touch Hugh.

Hugh leaped away, frightened, nearly falling. He drifted to the side of the track, to the inner grass, where he slid a bit. He could barely hold his balance. Joaquin's touch was like an electric shock to him.

Joaquin saw that Hugh slowed down, there was incomprehension in his face, maybe mixed with shock, but he was still running. Then he suddenly sped up again and tried to catch Joaquin.

Joaquin picked up his stuff from the bench—he knew he had no time to stop and dress; the clock was ticking. He got what he wanted. He smashed his clothes into the sports bag and ran toward the exit. He heard Hugh's steps from behind, but the man could not reach him. Hugh was bound by a relatively old body and could not compete with Joaquin's highly engineered young one.

After turning the corner, Joaquin could still hear, "Who are you? Stop! You have to tell me who you are!"

Joaquin received his second warning at that exact moment. He had so little time until the debarkation.

Hugh stopped beside the guard, panting heavily.

"Any trouble, sir?" asked the officer, looking at the man's distracted face.

"No . . . I mean . . . yes," he said, catching his breath, "I don't know . . . did you see . . . somebody leaving—a man?"

"Yes, I saw. He's a soldier, arrived before you, sir," said the guard. He looked at the scanner, "I have his ID number . . ."

"Only his ID number? No name? How can that be?" Hugh looked puzzled.

"You know there are people whose identity is kept—"

"OK, I see. I have to find him, do you understand?"

The guard looked as if he didn't understand at all. "If he did something unlawful you can report through your biochip and they will..."

"He didn't do anything bad... I mean, yes, he did."

"Did he hurt you, sir?" asked the officer, looking totally lost.

"No," said Hugh, helplessly shaking his head, and turned back to the stairs, "on the contrary..."

*

Joaquin changed in the taxi. He hoped that Hugh wouldn't call the police or the army after the shock he'd given him.

He felt a gentle satisfaction running through his body while he was trying to compose himself again. He took the long sleeve shirt, planning to leave the bag in the taxi; he wouldn't need it anymore. He closed his sweat glands as he'd learned in training; he wanted to be fresh and relaxed for the next encounter.

The luxury complex of the Bloom Hill Hospital was not far. He asked the taxi-driver to stop on the parking terrace at the second level and told him to wait. He knew that the second encounter would not take as long as the first, and he would have plenty of time for the last.

He asked directions at the nurse's desk—his special military ID left no doors closed for him. He hurried along the corridor and turned right at the end.

Taking off his raincoat in front of the door, he left it on the coat hanger. He dressed in a long, white apron above his usual clothes and put the toque on, which was folded in his pocket. He pressed the swinging door and entered the kitchen.

He bumped into a cook, whispered a silent sorry, and then went to the prepared breakfast on plates. He picked up the one with room number 402, and slid it professionally onto his palm. He wanted to serve the meal instead of the robots.

The visitors hadn't arrived yet and all those who stayed in the hospital with their relatives were still in their rooms. Cleaning robots drew wet lines on the corridors, assistant droids avoided them, floating between rooms. They were following some kind of organized dance, and Joaquin felt the hidden music behind it.

There was no visitor in the room. The woman—Katrina Pauwens, who was the second on Joaquin's list—was sitting in her bed with her eyes closed, leaning against the vertically set headrest. Her long, brown hair was carefully arranged against the pillow. Her hands lay close beside her body, palms down, perfectly placed. Disciplined beauty radiated from her.

Joaquin put the plate down as silently as he could. He didn't want to break the spell.

The walls held canvases painted with geometric forms in vivid colours and varying size. An easel stood at the corner with cleaned brushes drying in front. Formless remains of dried paint sat on a wooden palette. Each of these interesting and tangible objects called out for Joaquin to touch them.

The painting on the easel was unfinished. It was different from all the others, representing not a plane but a human figure. It obviously resembled a boy or a young man. His head was encircled with a halo and he pointed out from the picture towards to the viewer. It looked so real that Joaquin could almost shake his hand. This picture stood out from all the rest with its enchanting colours.

"Khm . . ." Joaquin was startled by the noise. Katrina cleared her throat, her eyes were open and she smiled at Joaquin.

"You're not a droid?" she asked, surprised.

Joaquin wanted to stick to his plan, so he didn't say a word. He picked up the plate and circled the bed. He placed a serviette in front of the women and lifted the lid from the plate. Katrina's face filled with happiness.

"Wonderful, thank you!" she said, taking the knife and fork. It seemed that she didn't care about Joaquin anymore. She cut the fried eggs into pieces and pushed them into a certain formation.

"Look at this!" she was enthusiastic and showed the geometric forms to him. "Unbelievable. I can't stop myself from creating things!"

Then she broke the design by starting to eat the pieces with a pleased smile on her face. She totally disregarded Joaquin as if he were part of the room. He tried to hide between the easel and the wall. All was white around him; the white bed sheet connected to the white bedframe, attached to the bright white paved floor—he had a fair chance of hiding in his white apron.

Katrina swallowed the last bite and pushed the plate away. Joaquin wanted to drag out the moment as long as possible, as if it were freshly prepared pasta, to enjoy the encounter more. But that moment eventually had to be ended. He wanted to go back to the origin of the moment, where he could find a timeless existence; God himself. For God, there was no time. But for humans, time was made of all these moments.

He took the plate while gently touching Katrina's hand. The woman suddenly looked at him, her pupils narrowing. She focused on Joaquin's face; her lips formed the mixture of a soft, affected, and surprised smile. Joaquin stepped back to the place he'd stood before, beside the canvas on the easel.

Katrina raised her hand and pointed at him, then to the painting. "That's you! Oh, God, you are..."

Joaquin did not see the similarity between himself and the figure on the canvas, but he felt a surprising attachment to it. This strange illusion might have come from the gesture, the hand pointing out of the frame. But the shower of memories that came after touching Katrina was real—it brought the memories of an unseen world into his mind, one that perhaps never even existed.

He hoped that was what he came for. Those ancient, past memories were what he was looking for, a life he had once been part of too. Sometime long ago.

He wished to stay and look at the woman more, but he still had one more name on the list. He might not even have enough time for the last encounter. The sun was already high above the clouds, shining down through the cumulus gathering over south New Jersey. Katrina felt that too, and she pushed away the bedclothes, just pulling her slippers on. When she finally stood up, he was already at the end of the corridor.

"Come back!" he heard the shout from behind. "I knew about you. You have to understand that I knew about you! Come back, please!"

Joaquin stopped for a moment. It was hard to hear the sobbing supplication, which echoed after him until he got into the taxi. He felt a poignant sadness for the first time in his life, and it told him that he was on the right track.

The taxi fell over the Big Disk's edge and descended back to the world of chaos. Back to the old Manhattan, where the last encounter awaited him.

There was an interview on the news channel in the car radio. Congresswoman and liberal democrat Katrina Pauwens, who had just undergone surgery after her accident, was speaking.

She said she was happy, that she'd completely regained her vision and that she could enjoy every moment of her life. All previous problems seemed so small now, especially in regard to her political career. As to the question of how she would vote for the "Military Law Package," including carrying guns again, she said she would vote contrary, definitely no.

*

The driver charged ten times the usual fare for taking him to the still-chaotic East Village. The police surrounded Tompkins Square Park, where those rebel units defending Soho and Downtown last week had been forced to pull back. The retreat was a painful, but necessary, decision for the anti-colonist leaders. But they could not escape anymore; the SWAT units of the North American Union together with the United Colony Special Forces held them in a chokehold.

The only hope for them was the twelve hostages they'd captured from New Cloud York. They'd entered with a skycar, using a modified stolen registration ID. Joaquin had seen the Big Disk's chief of security in the news the day before; he defended himself, saying he had no power to control the situation anymore due to external factors. He had to think about the coming war.

He'd found his third encounter—Trevor H. Cuningham, the leading hostage negotiator of the Disk—in this news program. Joaquin had found three of the seven names by just watching the news. That was lucky because he simply didn't have time to do a serious search.

Cuningham must have been living in the posh side of New Cloud York, but he'd had to leave his comfort zone and come down to the grime to pull his fellow citizens out of this deep shit. This shitstorm was caused by the neo-colonists—and the oligarchs behind them. They drilled down deep into the economy like a worm and killed the market. Asia had erupted and attacked the other continents; people started a new worldwide migration. The oligarchs—financing the neo-colonists—enjoyed the chaos.

It's not worth it, thought Joaquin; *this is not worth twelve lives.* The oligarchs wouldn't stop their doom-machines for these people.

Cuningham might be there in one of the armoured vehicles, behind the police cordon. Joaquin wanted to go inside the guarded area, and he hoped that his special ID would open the gate again.

The sun was high enough, it was already past eleven. He silenced the warning messages coming from his biochip, because he had made his decision; he would not go to the meeting point, he wouldn't rejoin his unit. He was taking a high risk; the guard could ask him, seeing his ID, why he didn't take his duffle bag and get the hell out of Manhattan, go to Asia to protect the world. He hoped the guard would be too busy to look at his embarkation date.

He was in luck; the guard just nodded and let him through the entry. Between the two lines of armoured attack vehicles, there was a foldable camp table with officers in uniform around it. They studied a huge, old paper map. Snipers and soldiers were all around: beside, below, and atop the vehicles, pointing their guns at the barricade made from furniture, street paving, and old burned cars. The anti-colonist's flag was waving atop the junk-wall with the sign of a capital A in the middle of the exploded Moon.

Joaquin stopped behind the group comprising twenty soldiers. He carefully pinned up his special ID. Only two of the policemen standing on the outer edge of the circle glanced towards him, but they held their gaze for several seconds. They would assume he was one of the experts from the antiterrorist group, which was strangely not far from the truth.

The leader of the SWAT group, a major according to the stars on his shoulder, commanded his men from the middle. Lieutenant Cuningham stood right next to him. His white, short sleeve shirt was crumpled from the hardship of his three-days-long negotiation. He wore the newest electronic shield built into his vest. His energy-weapon's grip stuck out from under his arm.

"This is your last chance, Trevor," said the major, pointing to the negotiator. "The first big assignment after your injury. I'm counting on you."

Trevor nodded with a clouded look. He was not as enthusiastic as his boss. He proficiently unstrapped his weapon from its holster and put it down on the table.

"You're going in unarmed?" asked the major, raising his eyebrows. "OK, it's your decision. But we only have one chance. The army's special forces will arrive this afternoon and blow this place sky-high, if you don't achieve anything. We already lost more than twelve men in Soho, so we don't want to waste any more time."

The group formed a corridor in font of Trevor. He fastened his vest's straps before leaving. His friends patted his back on the way to the two-storey-high barricade. He avoided the burning cars, the throttle, and the dark smoke coming from the flaming tyres. He didn't look back. He raised both hands and walked forward, stopping halfway to the barricade.

The sun went down behind the Big Disk, casting dark shadows over the park. Joaquin knew that the army was already looking for him, and it wouldn't take them long to find him. They were looking for him because the first wave of soldiers were on their way to the troop carriers. And they were looking for him because they had invested a lot of energy and money to train him as a special military agent.

But he didn't care about that. He only concentrated on the man fifteen metres from him, walking to the anarchist's barricade.

Suddenly a gap opened at one-and-a-half-storey height of the debris wall. A machine gun's barrel protruded out of it, and somebody gave orders through a megaphone. "Stay where you are! Turn around! We want to see that there are no weapons on your back."

Trevor did what the voice asked. After he made a slow full-circle, he pulled up his trousers leg to show he wasn't carrying a gun on his ankle.

"What do you want?" the question came as he faced the barricade again. "We didn't change our demands!"

"I know," shouted Trevor towards the wall. His voice echoed back from the surrounding houses for several seconds, "but we have to come to an agreement. You can't demand twelve innocent lives!"

"They are not innocent!" the voice brutally cut the silence. "They have undeniable responsibility for the present chaotic situation."

"They didn't cause the Asian conflict!" Trevor shouted back. The man behind the megaphone hesitated for a few seconds.

"We don't believe you! We don't believe anybody who comes from New Cloud York. Turn around and come back only when you've fulfilled our demands."

Trevor stayed. He started to unstrap his vest. "I'm taking this off to show my commitment to a serious negotiation! We can make a deal!"

This resistance must've made the anti-colonist spokesman angry, because the gunman shot a round beside Trevor. The negotiator swayed a bit, pulling his hands back around his body, then straightened them into the air again.

"Don't shoot! You have to believe me, we will find a solution!" he shouted and dropped his vest to the ground.

The major hissed nervously and shook his head. He obviously didn't like what was happening, but instructed everybody to stay ready and silent.

"I don't know why you think those twelve are the cause of the Solar System-wide crises. You can't believe that the new power in Asia confederated with those people to turn the world upside down! You can't really believe that if you keep them captive, then New China will retreat its army and the economy will miraculously recover! You're just helping those oligarchs push the world into anarchy!" Trevor said, passionately, and took a few more steps towards the barricade.

There was another round of shots, but this time one caught Trevor's leg. He collapsed in pain. The reply came immediately from the SWAT unit; a shower of energy beams covered the anarchist's post from every manned gun.

"Cease fire, for God's sake, everybody!" commanded the major. "Somebody go and bring him back!"

Joaquin had raced to help him before the major finished his sentence. While he was running, emotions engulfed him, though he'd never cried before.

At that moment, the barricade became a fortress; hundreds of gun barrels pointed out at him from small portholes. When the hail erupted, he covered Trevor's body with his own. The negotiator lay on his back and struggled to take a breath. When Joaquin tore off his shirt, he saw blood streaming from a deep wound on Trevor's right lung. It was a deadly shot.

Joaquin saw then the long scar in the middle of the man's chest, cutting through the sternum. He put his right hand below Trevor's head, the left over his heart.

Trevor's pupils widened. He wanted to say something, but only blood—dark as the night sky—came out of his mouth. Joaquin's tears were falling on the man's face, he wanted desperately to read the last words from the blood-covered lips.

"You are ... you ..."

Joaquin saw Trevor's life playing before his eyes like an imaginary movie with strangely mixed pictures. He felt a close relationship with the personality appearing in that film, although it was clear that it was somebody else's life. But he sensed the friendship, the bizarre attachment they'd had with each other. Trevor was standing, smiling in this common life-film; his eyes filled with understanding and gratitude. He radiated peace; never-ending peace, filling everything.

Then Trevor's heart beat its last.

The steel bullet got Joaquin on his side. He wouldn't regain consciousness even when the special forces finally arrived and raided the place, burning down the park and sacrificing twelve lives—though saving thousands of others—for an unknown and incomprehensible future.

*

Colonel Richard Mortensen, the Asian Allied Forces' chief of science, visited the military hospital to see the operation to save Joaquin's life. Ruth Baumgartner, the army's leading psychologist called him down from his office, because she had a couple of important and sensitive announcements about their patient.

"What do you mean, the case is more than remarkable?" asked the colonel looking suspiciously to his officer.

"I mean that we had some good surprises along with the bad ones."

"You call it a surprise that the subject of our multimillion dollar project became a deserter?"

"OK, maybe you won't see it as a surprise. But it's interesting to me why he did it."

"Why does a clone desert?" asked the colonel with a strange gesture.

"He's not a simple clone; he is one of the special ones—he's a 'lost soul.' In his original body, he died on the streets of Jersey's poor district, where our local agent found him. He captured his soul with the soul-trap. We had no information about his identity, so we gave him one."

"37L2328, if I remember his original name correctly. He called himself Joaquin, as I was told."

"Yes, your info is correct," nodded Ruth. "I spoke with him forty-seven times during his training. He initiated the name; I accepted."

"You had no other choice," grumbled Mortensen and smoothed down his grey hair, "than to accept it. Don't change the subject; why didn't he come to the rendezvous point?"

"This is a hospital registration list," answered Ruth handing over the paper.

"This is a transplantation list," said the colonel, shocked.

"Specifically, it's a list about illegal transplants."

"Why do you think it's illegal?"

"Look," said the psychologist, annoyed, "we don't need to pretend that we don't know anything about the trade of illegal organs. There is an existing market and demand for this in Manhattan. 37L2328—Joaquin's birth body—was a victim of that."

The colonel looked at the paper for a few seconds. "I see. He wanted to find them. Like a personal revenge. He found all those who bought his organs. It's clear."

"I think you're wrong. It's not clear at all. But this recording may make it clearer. He said this in one of our sessions."

"Where is the key to our identity?" they could hear Joaquin's voice from the Dictaphone. "I start off with a clean slate, but why don't I remember anything?"

"Did he look for himself?" asked the colonel, looking through the window, where Joaquin was being operated on. "Did he want to find his own identity in the transplanted people?"

"Yes," nodded the woman. She held a long, significant pause. "You have to let me continue my work with him."

If the colonel could throw fire with his eyes, he would burn his colleague to ashes. "You are insane. We've spent an unbelievable amount of money to change him into a perfect soldier, a perfect military agent."

"You have to understand, we are so close to knowing more about the secret origin of the human soul—"

"What more do you want to know?" the colonel turned angrily away. "We've used the clone technology efficiently for years now, and we've proven that the soul exists without the body. What more do you need?"

"What more? I need an explanation why those people with transplanted organs changed their character. Why the fat, lazy lobbyist, Hugh Kingdon, changed to a sportsman after getting Joaquin's lung . . ."

"Why, why? . . . Because he got a new chance, he gave up smoking and wanted to live a healthy life!"

"And why did he turn to be a pacifist from the leadership of the arms lobby? That's not a physical attribution—"

"Oh, c'mon," the colonel stopped her harshly. "We can't win the war with scientific theories! The world is on fire out there, and you want to continue your study!"

There was a knock at the door. An officer entered with a communicator in his hand. He saluted then handed it over to Ruth. She started to speak with somebody.

"Yes, good day, Mrs. Pauwens. I understand your feelings. No. I don't think you've gone mad . . . . We should meet to speak about this . . . yes, it is remarkable. I think it puts the story in a different perspective . . . yes, I'll call you."

The colonel was looking rigidly at Ruth. He knew what would happen next. The psychologist started speaking, "Mrs. Pauwens said that she lost her vision in an accident, but after an optic nerve transplant, not only did it restore her sight, but it changed her life. She was a supporter of the war, now she is against it. She said that a man visited her. According to the security cameras, that man was Joaquin—the scanners recorded his ID. She said that when he touched her, she saw pictures from somebody else's life. It was strange but familiar too."

The colonel handed back the list. "Does this mean I have to give up on him?"

"In the name of science, yes. You're the chief of science in the army, you have to do it."

He shook his head in resignation. "All right. But you'll have to explain this to the United Colony Army Training Centre. We'll be losing one of our most sophisticated military machines."

The woman was already stepping back from the open door. "You might think that he's only a machine, but I'll tell you one more thing—Hugh Cuningham was the third on the list. According to his old boss, he was a tough guy, a hard-line cop driven by his emotions and passions. He was severely wounded in a raid and had been in a coma for three weeks. After his recovery, he became a hostage negotiator. Do you realize what a big change that is? A man who was unable to make even a simple compromise took a job to represent other people's interests, to negotiate!"

"And which organ did he get from 37L2328?"

The woman stared at him with a "what-do-you-think" look. "His heart."

Colonel Mortensen looked at his soldier lying beyond the glass wall. He could not decide what was the biggest loss; the time, the money, or the chance to try him in real, warlike circumstances.

But, after all, it was science—that very strange, intangible thing—that had given the army this miraculous invention. And so he had to support these experiments. What choice did he have?

In the end, he had thirty-eight other, specially trained clones. They were already on their way out to enemy lines.

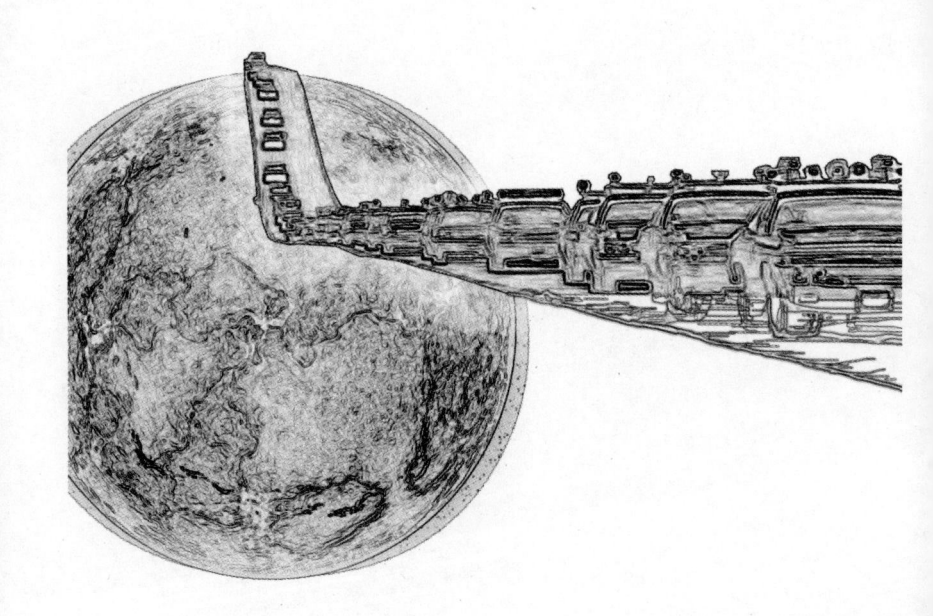

* This montage created by the author using element of the pursuit scene from the movie
The Sugarlenad Express - Universal Pictures 1974

XI.

Eastern-European Express

Jonathan put more pressure on the barrel of his gun. "I've had enough of your tricks. Finish, or you die."

He needed to make everything crystal clear after the cop had taken back manual control and made that five-hundred-meter freefall with the flying police car. Jonathan had been able to restore the autopilot once they finally finished the scuffle, then the aircar climbed back to the skyway heading west.

Emese looked down to the dirty-grey line of the river Danube flowing between the narrow gaps of the sky-houses. Then she noticed their pursuers from the rear camera's picture.

"You idiot, you called your partners!" she said in Hungarian, yanking the policeman's uniform.

"What did you say to him? Speak in English," Jonathan spat. They'd deleted all the damn software extensions in his biochip, including translation, while he was being processed at the jail. How was he supposed to know what she was saying?

They'd thrown him into prison for *infringing the quota law*–meaning he had sex with Emese without contraceptives, for which he could get a minimum of three years in Eastern Europe. Though he only had a year and a half left, Emese had persuaded him to escape. That was three days ago. Jonathan still stank, having crawled through the sewage system. He'd applied for cleaning and gotten the task due to his good behaviour. He wasn't really a bad kid, but sometimes he couldn't control his passions.

They headed north from the Big Plain. Jonathan had lifted a four-wheeler—they had found weapons in it. It was a hunter's car, the owner must have come from the Big Plain National Park, they reckoned. While the hunter went into the loo, Jonathan had stolen his car.

There were some clothes in the car too—that was why Jonathan was in deep-green camouflaged hunter trousers—and it was full of petrol, enough to get them to Budapest's border. The tank was empty by the time they reached the South Railway Bridge, though, so they pushed the four-wheeler into the river.

Then they continued on foot until the next refuelling tower. They climbed up the fire escape, not wanting to use the lift, because the police had surely issued a warrant for his arrest. The Kecskemet Regional Correctional Institution had probably sent out dogs to catch him.

Jonathan hadn't wanted to steal a skycar; he knew he couldn't break through the intricate security system of retina and bio scanners. So Emese pretended to faint next to one of the charging poles where a police car had stopped just a moment before. A young policeman immediately jumped out to help the girl. He seated her in the front. In a flash, Jonathan grabbed his weapon. He couldn't pull it out, though, because the holster was electronically defended. It was much easier for the policeman—the weapon had been activated by the touch of his hand.

Jonathan fought for the gun and pushed the policeman's finger on the trigger; the energy-shot went through the officer's leg.

Jonathan refused to let the cop—Peter, according to the dashboard ID—collapse. He held him up with one hand while turning the weapon and the policeman's hand back against his ribs with the other. Emese climbed into the backseat and Jonathan forced Peter to slide into the other side.

It was a bizarre situation with the weapon. They flew for a while like that—the cop's twisted hands with the gun, Jonathan's palm on Peter's hand, holding the trigger with his finger—but Peter's wound grew worse, so he turned off the personalized defence and gave the gun to Jonathan.

Then the policeman wanted to know about their plan, but the youngsters only demanded to go to Frankfurt. Peter instructed the computer and asked permission to deal with his wound. He took a healing capsule from the glove box and poured its contents into the wound. The energy blast hadn't been too destructive, it passed through without touching the veins. After a few hours, he would be better.

But just when everything and everybody looked calm and relaxed, the cop pushed the control stick forward. The skycar's nose dipped then stalled—the *antigrav* engines pulling the police car to the ground. They fell towards the Danube, fighting and punching each other, when finally Jonathan pushed the button for autopilot. The *antigrav* engines changed their polarization again and kept them on a safe level above the river. They were dangerously close, enough to see their own mirrored reflection on the metallic, shiny surface of the water.

"The stalling triggered an automatic alarm, but I've also sent a signal from my biochip to the centre," said the policeman, nodding to the line of red-blue lights behind them. "You can't really hope that you'll get away with it."

"Tell him he should stop speaking Hungarian," Jonathan's voice was threatening.

"No Hungarian, do you understand?" Emese yanked again on the officer's uniform, although it was she who had started speaking in her mother tongue first.

"And no new tricks, I've had enough!" said Jonathan, knocking on the controls. "I'm taking over the driving too."

Peter laughed. "An uneducated immigrant who has nothing, no ID, no driving licence, no residence? You're not in the database, so the car computer would reject you!"

"It won't if you convince it to let me drive."

Jonathan had no idea if the policeman was telling the truth or not; he had never driven an aircar before—much less a police car. The cop stayed silent, so Jonathan didn't bring up the idea of driving again. Let the autopilot fly instead.

They had followed the Danube to the northwest. There were big cities—an overgrown megapolis—below them now. Its inhabitants had nearly sucked the river dry for its energy. Not much water was left anyway after the global Big Heat. The fusion reactors, which broke the water down to its components, extended deep into the riverbed. House boats were anchored around them, trying to tap the steam and use it to satisfy their energy demands. This was the energy of the poor, called steam stealers. They were barely tolerated deadbeats with their rafts made of waste wood.

The global heat reigned for two-hundred-and-twenty years, then crisp cold returned from the northwest. The mountaintops of Transylvania were once again covered with snow, but the Carpathian basin became a frosty desert. The cold broke at the *cold-heat division line*—simply called the *Cold Line*—beyond the river Danube, the extreme heat reigned.

The acclimatized cities, like Wien-Budapest—the long, stretching megapolis—weren't as affected by the climatic change. The only indicator for them was the realization of how much more they were consuming. The large *Fusion Reactor Towers* revealed their hunger was inexhaustible.

They had just passed the reactors when one of the chasing police cars flew alongside them. The driver had been hiding in the steam, so Jonathan hadn't seen them coming. The two aircars bounced against each other for a second.

"Piss off! Get lost!" Shouted Jonathan, frightened, and pushed the weapon to Peter's head.

"Start to descend!" they heard from the chasers. "You have no chance to leave the Eastern Region!"

Jonathan was puzzled; he looked at the other car, then back to his hostage.

"He's right," said Peter, relaxed. "They've already drawn up an electromagnetic shield at the Wien border. We'll drop like a dead fly."

"Climb!" exclaimed Jonathan. "We have to go above it!"

The cop looked flabbergasted. "It won't work. The aircar's maximum is three thousand, the wall goes up to five thousand."

"I don't care, then we'll set a new record," Jonathan looked determined.

Emese was rather frightened. "Jonathan, he's right. Better to turn south."

"We're not going south. We need to be there on time, or don't you want to?"

Emese pulled her leg up, holding it with her hand like a kid. "Yes I do. Do as you want," she agreed.

Jonathan nodded. "Climb! Right now," he said. He was peremptory but calm.

Peter pulled the control stick so that the aircar shot up in a coarse pitch. The chasers were lost in the duel and left behind, then descended strongly. They followed them in a wedge shape down below.

When Emese looked back, she noticed other vehicles behind the police lines. Quite a big group had gathered and was following them. One aircar left the group, sped up, and tried to reach them.

"Look! They came from a news channel!" she exclaimed excitedly and tried to spell out the letters on the car. "Global News, Jonathan, it's GN!" her emotions were running high.

"Maybe they'll help us . . ." Jonathan murmured, although he was not looking enthusiastic.

The GN aircar finally reached them. There was a transparent bubble on the top of the vehicle, where the news agents and reporters could easily follow the situation. A pretty woman appeared there. She prepared herself while a text appeared on the side of the car, stating they wanted to interview them.

"Open a communication channel to them," demanded Jonathan while the policeman connected to the news car.

"Hello, I'm Sally Heisinger, the leading reporter of GN Eastern Europe. We've received your message that you want to give an interview."

Jonathan looked reproachfully at Emese. "Did you call them? I didn't agree to that."

"I know," Emese cast her eyes down, "but we can profit from it, as you've said before!"

"Can we start?" asked the reporter, interrupting the increasingly heated discussion.

"Yes, no problem. Ask whatever you want," chirped the girl happily. She leaned towards the side window and waved.

Light came up in the bubble, the reporter adjusted her hair, and stuck her best smile on her face. "Hello, I'm Sally Heisinger, with an exceptional exclusive report over the river Danube. I have a chance to interview Eastern Europe's most wanted fugitives: Jonathan Pilgrim and Emese Honti. Their story isn't unique in this part of Europe, but they are the first to go against the existing legislation."

"We didn't go against it, that's bullshit," fretted Jonathan. "We just fell in love, that's all."

"Then why did you ask for right of asylum in Eastern Europe if you agree with the law?"

"I lost my job; I had no future in the West. I needed a change."

"I can understand your reasoning, as the job market got saturated. Was it worth it to lose your ID for a job? You became a ghost, all your personal files have been deleted in the West. You have to build up everything from scratch."

"I didn't care about that. My parents were American refugees, so I just continued what they started," answered Jonathan.

"If I'm right, they disembarked with the *New Mayflower* along with the *Naturals*."

"Yes, you're right."

"For those who don't know who the *Naturals* are, they are regarded as a sect. Their offspring are not genetically modified. Mr. Pilgrim, do you know that the Eastern Region Government introduced zero tolerance against the *Naturals*?"

"I am from a *natural* family too!" shouted Emese from the back. "We live over the *Cold Line*, in the mountains. It's still not a sin to be natural there."

"You're wrong, ma'am," said Peter, interrupting. "The law of the United Colony Council applies to you just as much as the others. The Transylvania Region is part of the European Confederation."

"And it's a sin if you break the quota and the *zero tolerance law*," the reporter took back control of the interview. "In the

West, you—as a *Natural*—can't have a child. Was that the real reason you got together? To create some kind of genetic revolution?"

Jonathan shook his head in disbelief. "What is this shit? I don't care about genetics. We only wanted to live a normal life."

"You could live sterilized in the South German Megapolis, in the Munchen-Stuttgart-Frankfurt-Nurnberg Region, where you might find a good job."

Jonathan shot an angry glance at the camera situated on the end of the telescopic arm.

"Do you have a child?" asked Emese, pushing both hands to the window. The camera wiggled to focus on her, trying to find the girl's face behind her fingers. "What would you do for your child?"

Then, suddenly, the news car left them alone. Emese thought they'd run away because of her impudent question, but the real reason was looming in front of them; the electromagnetic border fence flickered a fluorescence orange in the light rain.

"We won't make it," said Peter, forcing the aircar higher. The control stick was shaking in his hand, showing that the floater had already reached its maximum altitude. The top of the virtual wall was nowhere in sight; it disappeared into the faded grey clouds.

"I'm slowing down," said the policeman and pulled back on the stick.

Jonathan placed his hand above Peter's and pushed forward again. "No way," he said.

Emese looked at them, frightened. The chasers had stayed behind, they were the only ones racing to the middle of the magnetic net.

They'd all prepared for the worst when, at the last minute, the artificial border disappeared. At the same time the police chief of Western Region's voice broke the silence from the radio.

"All right, son, start descending. From this point, we'll escort you. No sudden, dumb ideas, no reckless manoeuvers."

Peter started to descend to an average flight altitude. On both sides of their flight path, police aircars lined up and joined in behind them. News cars and private floaters followed the hundreds of blue-red lights in seemingly endless waves. There were flying cars from human rights activists and organizations. Some of them towed huge banners or wrote messages in the clouds with colored lasers.

"Look!" exclaimed Emese. "*We are with you!*" she read aloud from one of the banners. "*We don't need superhumans! Superhuman equals overpopulation!*" she read from others. "What an enormous crowd of aircars! They've shut down the East-West highway for us!"

"Big damn hype for nothing!" said Jonathan.

"Without them you would be in custody again," chided Emese.

"Tune to a news station to see what's going on," she instructed Peter.

Peter did what she requested, and they could see the ocean of vehicles behind them. The red and blue police lights painted the clouds above Wien-Budapest, reflecting back from the tinted glass panels of Wien's sky-towers. People were standing on the roofs, holding handwritten banners. Somebody had painted a fetus with a bleeding heart on one of the flat roofs.

"Look, I did it!" Emese clapped her hands in happiness. "I asked for support by sending four thousand messages about our plan after your escape. Give me some credit for this!"

"Well done," murmured Jonathan. "But tell me, how do you plan the future with this cortege?"

Emese's eyes rounded. "Like we discussed, we'll go to the Frankfurt Space Terminal and stop them from taking Jack away. From there we head to the *Free Zone*."

Jonathan sighed deeply. "Do you really think they'll just let us take Jack back from the foster parents?"

Emese looked at the rear camera's picture, and suddenly she was not so confident anymore.

"They're our guards," she pointed to the civilian aircars spreading around them like a handheld fan. "They won't let it happen."

"They let it happen with the *New Mayflower*. They've voted for the Law of Quota, they've pushed you and me to the periphery of society."

"The Law of Quota was implemented against overpopulation . . ."

"No! That law only served the needs of the *superhumans* and clone technology, which led to congestion!" Jonathan interrupted angrily. "There is no sickness, no ageing. Only *Zero Tolerance* for the *Naturals*.

Emese lost heart. She thought it had been a good idea to involve the public in their cause. She didn't say anything for a while, staring at the bare, snowless mountaintops of the Alps below. There were sand lands down there, deserts interrupted by circular, green oases with the only remains of fertile soil. The farms connected to the cities cultivated the main products on soilless plantations to fulfil the food demands of the overgrown population now. They made fusion reactors in all the rivers—demolishing the dams, which were not used due to the lack of water caused by the heat. These towers were blowing their steam into the stratosphere where the natural phenomenon—the Big Heat—dissolved it.

"Do you have a child?" Emese suddenly asked the policeman.

Peter pulled up a picture on the dashboard's touchscreen. There were two little girls, smiling.

"The bigger one is Judit, she will be nine soon, the smaller one is Gerda, three."

"So you could have two children . . . ?"

"The officials are required to go through the genetic treatment. All *law-abiding* citizens have a chance for a bigger family."

"But we can have only one in the East Region."

"Government employees can have two."

"The future law-abiding citizens . . ." added Jonathan sarcastically.

"Do you believe in God?" asked Emese after a short pause.

"Why do you want to know?" asked Peter. "Maybe I do, maybe I don't, either way I have to follow the law."

"And what about God's rule? About the freedom of birth, about the priority of God's created lives?" asked Emese. "Why do I live? According to society's rules, I have no right to have offspring."

"That's not true. They've introduced this only to keep the birth rate at a reasonable level . . ."

"Damn birth control!" said Jonathan heatedly. "What kind of birth control is it when government officials can have more than one baby?"

When they stopped talking, the Frankfurt Spaceport was already close ahead. Spaceships—gleaming like flashy, silver spots—departed from the three massive towers, and broke through the clouds of smog, heading to the colonies. The Space Terminal was situated to the left of the departure terminals, so Jonathan instructed Peter to aim for that building.

"We won't reach them in time," said Jonathan, looking at his watch. He didn't say anything to Peter as he pushed the aircar to the limit.

Suddenly civilian aircars left the chasing crowd and sped up towards the departure towers. They formed a colourful armada in front of the greyish background. Only the police continued the chase.

"Look, you fool!" said Jonathan pointing to them, when they reached the terminal. The supporting crowd of aircars blocked the prohibited airspace over the departure. Peter tuned to the space control frequency.

"We've closed the airspace on all terminals. No departure for . . ."

"They're helping us! Their ship can't depart!" exulted Emese. "The whole world is with us!"

Peter arrived in front of the main building at high speed. The police had already opened a path for them to land safely on the platform. Thousands of supporters were standing, waving behind the cordons on both side of the entrance.

"Get out and do as I say; no tricks!" said Jonathan, gripping Peter's neck. Emese went first to the huge glass door of the terminal.

There was an even bigger crowd inside. They didn't see a cordon or other officials, police or security guards. They passed through the human corridor, everyone holding hands and pointing them in the right direction. Thousands of supporters touched them and shook their hands, giving them courage to continue.

The living corridor led them to a real one, where spaceport personnel were waiting for them.

"This way. It's shorter," they said smiling, showing the way then closed the door behind them.

Peter used this disruptive event for a quick counterattack; he spun and disarmed Jonathan.

Jonathan kneaded his hand painfully. "So is this the end?" he asked.

Peter didn't say anything. He closed the firing system, so Jonathan couldn't use it anymore, and gave it back to him.

"I'm not ending anything. But I want us to finish this adventure on equal terms," answered Peter. There was firm understanding in his eyes.

Jonathan put his arm back, but more gently this time. He was not angry at the cop anymore.

The corridor ended at the newly built Interstellar Space Terminal. But there was no cheering and supporting crowd on the other side, only families. Men and women with one or two children, waiting for their flight.

"We're looking for Jack Pilgrim's foster parents!" shouted Jonathan. His voice echoed against the walls and the huge windows.

"I'm Jonathan Pilgrim, his father!"

The people stayed back, frightened; children ran behind their parents. Some looked around to see if anyone came forward.

An elderly woman and a man with grey hair stepped out from the background. They followed the random path between the packages. There was a sling wrapped across her chest. Two tiny legs and arms stuck out below the cheerful stripes.

Emese burst into tears. She hurried to the couple, but they were just standing there, puzzled. Emese ran the last few metres and started to free the baby from the sling. The woman caught her wrist to stop her, so Jonathan put the weapon to Peter's head.

"Give the baby to her or I'll kill him!"

The foster mother loosened the knot around her neck and let the baby out of the wrap. Emese immediately took her boy back.

Jack woke up for only a few seconds, then laid his head onto his mother's shoulder.

"Come stand next to me!" she called to Jonathan.

Nobody looked scared around them. They didn't protest. Their worn eyes were darkened with resignation. Nobody wanted to be a hero or do something stupid. It looked like they had all experienced this kind of excitement before.

"Where do you plan to go?" asked Jack's foster father. He had long, untidy hair, and his sweater and coat were ragged and aged. Hand-sewn patches faded on his trousers. His outfit was well-matched to this bizarre, riff-raff company.

Jonathan clasped Emese's arm and backed off towards the door.

"It's none of your business. Far from here, where they won't bother us..."

"There is no place like that out there," said the foster mother calmly.

Jonathan erupted with all his repressed tension. "You're lying!" he shouted. "We're going to the *Free Zone*. Nobody will stop a police car!"

The old man took two steps towards them. He raised his hands defensively. "Please, believe us," he said gently. "This is the *Free Zone*."

"You're just saying that to stop us and take our boy on the next flight with you," Emese spat in anger. She held her boy more tightly.

"Please..." begged the man, "believe us! We aren't going anywhere from here. This is the closed sector of the Interstellar Terminal. This is the *Free Zone*, the no man's land—"

"Bullshit!" shouted Jonathan. "It's all over the news, that they take the natural children to an exoplanet where they make a new colony..."

The old man opened his arms. "My name is Hans. We are all *Naturals*. One of the human rights organisation helped us to come here. They organised your child's adoption too, because the mother was an outlaw and the father was in prison. Everybody thinks that the *Naturals* leave the Earth from here. The officials use the pretence to keep the public quiet."

Emese and Jonathan looked around. They were embarrassed for a while, but finally understood the situation. The torn clothes, the line of mattresses beside the windows, the trash piles next the bins... everything became clear.

"We've been living here for six months, waiting for a person sent by God to take us out of here."

Emese still looked disbelieving. "We still have undisturbed areas. Transylvania has big forests..."

"The long arm of the law can reach you everywhere. We can't go to the East, the cold and the war comes from there," said somebody from the crowd.

"We survived many wars and cold before—" answered Emese.

"If you leave here, they'll arrest you and take away your child again," said Hans. "Confirm it," he turned to Peter, who nodded.

"But there are those people who supported us . . ." tried Jonathan.

"Yes. They were there to help you and lead you here in safety. This is the new Interstellar Terminal, which is not under the law of the European Confederation or even the United Colony. From here we can fly to the exoplanets someday, if there is no war. Or if someone financed further construction and flights."

Jonathan had to face that the man was telling the truth. After Wien, everything had been smooth and unproblematic, as they'd planned. The police had fallen under the influence of public opinion and human rights activists to let them reach the Space Terminal.

"Go," said Jonathan to Peter, releasing him. He guarded Peter until they reached the corridor and then placed the gun to the floor. With a slight kick, he sent it back to the policeman. He knew that Peter wouldn't do anything; the cop had had plenty of opportunity already.

"Good luck," said Peter, jogging in the opposite direction.

Jonathan watched him disappear around the corner, back to his well-controlled life. Back to the world of genetically engineered people, to his wife with her perfect, ideal body, not prone to weight gain, to his comfortable, sterile life with no sickness and with the span of one-hundred-twenty years...

The place where he had wanted to be at times, before...

Before he met Emese.

She pulled him back to the *Free Zone*, among the Naturals.

And there they would stay until a rich patron came to establish the Colony of the Free-born on one of the exoplanets...

Or until God would come to judge this *perfect* world...

Stephen Paul Thomas's other novels:
Cluster

Will be soon available in printed and e-book format (2014)
Articity SF

The skybus raced haplessly towards its inevitable fate on the Mars New Home Colony. An old cop saves the passengers from death... but this is only the beginning.

Alex Sverlov regains consciousness in the middle of the Indian Ocean with his leg tied to an anchor rope... but this is only the beginning.

A new world power arises. The New China Empire conquered Asia in two regional atomic wars and is taking its place on the world stage... but this is only the beginning.

The M-epidemic starts to spread around the inhabited colonies in the Solar System... but this is still only the beginning of the story.

In this stunning and intricate conspiracy SF novel, the main characters find themselves in the cluster of a Solar System-wide epidemic, while even more powerful physical and spiritual forces are pulling the strings of their lives behind the scenes.

A new world, a new epidemic, but the conflicts are the same.

You can only find out more about it if you place yourself into the middle of a cluster!

Stephen Paul Thomas's new novel:
The Seed I.
There Are Other Worlds
coming soon in printed and e-book format (2015)
Articity SF

    A few years after the events of Cluster, a delegation arrives at the Mars New Home Colony to celebrate the three-hundred-year anniversary of the Martian colonies. Many illustrious guests take part in the event. Among them is the hero of Mars—one of the founding fathers of the Martian colonies—Maximilian Kilbraun, returning to his beloved red planet after many long years of living on Earth. Frederic Bomont, the famous exobiologist, arrives on the same ship. He wants to conduct genetic research to find out why the astronauts of the famous Mission Twelve—like Max, who's celebrating his one hundred fiftieth birthday—can live such long and healthy lives without genetic modification. Julia Tot, the rowdy sculptor, joins his investigation as she embarks on her new ex-terra task; she's creating a sculpture on the main square for the tricentenary. Fred's genetic puzzle soon enlarges to a planet-wide quest when he finds the old video recording of the early private mission, the One Way to Mars. Meanwhile, Max's life becomes a nightmare; a strange madness begins to possess him. Everyone around him is haunted by a horrifying dream—an alien is seeking their lives.

    Although The Seed begins with the last pages of Cluster, it is an independent, exciting, and captivating SF novel that keeps you on the edge until the last page . . . and saves some secrets for the next part too.